jar
of
fire
flies

jar
of
fire
flies

A Collection
of Poems
to Brighten
Your Day

Written and Illustrated by
KARL ROSKAMP

Printed in the United States of America

First Edition: January 2019
10 9 8 7 6 5 4 3 2 1

Library of Congress Control Number: 2019900005

ISBN: 978-0-578-41387-7

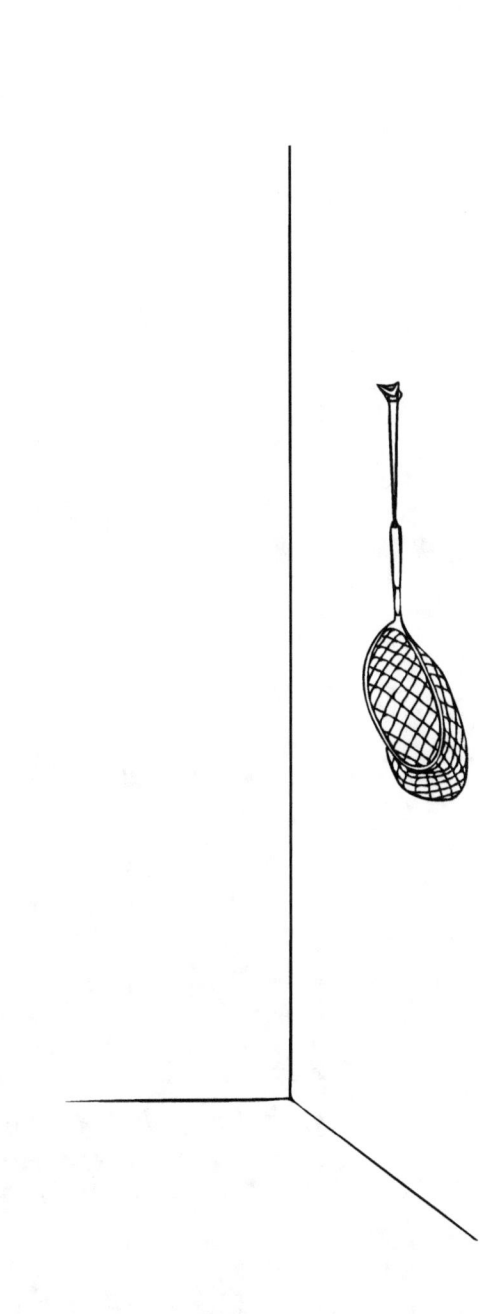

Introduction

Hello reader. Or more specifically, hello mom. Whether you bought this book because you enjoy poetry or somehow mistook my name for Karl Rove's, thank you. If you are reading this at the library, because you dislike paying for books, thank you to you too.

Before we start, let's make one thing clear. This is no ordinary poetry book. If you are expecting prose like William Shakespeare or Sylvia Plath, this book is probably not for you. You won't find complex narratives or extended metaphors here. Most of the poems can be taken at face value. When I talk about cheeseburgers, I mean cheeseburgers. I'm not using cheeseburgers as a symbol for excessive American consumerism and corporate greed. Though that is a good idea. (Note to self: write screenplay set in a cheeseburger-centric dystopia.)

We live in a world where attention is at a premium. With so much content available and so little time to consume it, it's important to create things that are thoughtful and compelling; not just listicles telling you which Disney princess you are. For better or worse, that is the way of the world. This selective attention, headline-consuming culture is what I had in mind when I wrote this book. It's why my poems are short and to the point.

This is not to say my poems are non-substantive. They are superstantive. Each poem is a nugget of thoughtfulness wrapped inside a creative presentation. This is a similar methodology to the one I used when I worked as a television reporter. I sought to give viewers something entertaining, even when the content was not. This often meant weaving in as many engaging stand ups and witty word plays as possible into my stories. Eventually though, I realized television reporting is not as glamorous as it seems and quit.

That is unless you consider covering city council meetings and local crop yields glamorous.

After reporting, I found that I still wanted to tell stories with a creative flare. This book was the perfect solution. I hope you see this creative passion in all my poems. If not, I fucked up big time.

Now you are probably wondering what to expect from this book. That is unless we are 500 years in the future, I've become a famous writer, and you're buying this as part of an anthology set. Assuming it's not the latter, here are answers to some of your potential questions.

What is this book about?

I am banking on no one reading the preface, so I'll tell you. It's about life and my exploration of the micro and macro-moments that compose it. I wanted to find relatable experiences and examine them through a humorous lens whether that is through poems, short writings, or lists. My goal is to tap into universal experiences and present them in a genuine and entertaining way.

Now you are probably thinking, "Karl, life is such an expansive subject. There's no way you can cover it all." You're right. This book is simply my take. It is my attempt to put the world into words. Years from now my perspective may change. I may even disagree with things I've written here. Or maybe I'll look back and realize how wise I was in my early 20s. Unlikely, but possible.

What inspired you to write this book?

I have always enjoyed writing. I find Instagram captions an opportunity to flex creativity. I write funny birthday cards for friends. I simply enjoy the opportunity to write in a way that is witty and humorous. Combine that with my lack of patience to write a traditional novel, and you have this book.

Tell us about your roots? Have you always wanted to be a poet?

My roots are amazing. Thank you Head and Shoulders. (Note to editor: please see if Head and Shoulders will compensate me for namedropping.) Also, no. I don't even consider myself a poet. I'm just like to make stuff and show it off, like first time parents.

The fact that I enjoy writing poetry is a miracle in itself. Both of my parents are chemistry PhDs. To them, writing poetry is as appealing as being a pilot with a fear of heights. Chemistry however is the guac to their burrito. I like to imagine they had many meals by Bunsen burner light while dating, probably discussing divalent germanium and tin in organic synthesis. Despite our differences, this book would not be possible without them. My parents have always been supportive of my ambitions. I'm sure if my childhood dream were to be a tree, my parents would have supported that too, though with silent disappointment. So thank you Mom and Dad for making this possible and thank you for not letting me be a tree.

What is your writing process like?
   Pretty boring. Next.

C'mon. What is your writing process like?
   Really? Well if you insist. I am constantly searching for interesting ideas. These ideas can be about anything. Take my poem "Ümlaüts" for instance. When an umlaut it placed over a "u," it looks like a smiley face. See: ü? This was a major epiphany. After I realized this, I tested the concept with different formats to find the best way to communicate the idea. This creative process manifested itself in myriad ways; including, but not limited to: 1) pacing in circles 2) staring stoically into the distance 3) checking Twitter and 4) eating Ben and Jerry's. Once I got the idea on paper, I tinkered with it until I love it. Or, in the case of some ideas, until I hate it so much I discard it.

My son is disappointed that I gave him a gift card to Applebee's for his graduation present instead of a new car. I want to make it up to him, but he has already read all of Shel Silverstein and Bo Burham's books. Is this the next best thing?
   Well, I don't want to compare myself to Shel and Bo, but I hope so. I have a considerable poetry pedigree. I studied classics at Harvard and after graduating I was published in various literary journals. Years later, I moved to Walden Pond to perfect my craft. I lived there for two years, eventually penning my magnum opus.

If this sounds like the life of Henry David Thoreau, well, that's a coincidence. Shel and Bo are tremendous though. Major influences too. It's an honor to be mentioned in the same sentence as them even if I wrote it.

I skimmed a few pages and my gut tells me this is not for me. Why should I keep reading?

That queasiness you're feeling is probably because you had gas station sushi for lunch. I recommend antacids. This book has something for everyone. Humor, comedy, funny observations, you name it. Seriously though, this book is more well-rounded than Santa Claus on Christmas Day. Unless you have an allergy to reading poetry, you'll be fine.

Why computer won't work. What do I do?

Wrong book! Have you tried turning it on and off though?

The Intro

Hello, I'm Karl and I hope you like poems.
I'm a beginner and I hope you like poems.

Where the Sidewalk Begins

Where the sidewalk begins
Anything goes,
Because what lies ahead
Nobody knows.
You can make your own path
If you dream big.
Dream of time travel, robots,
Or wings on a pig.
Dream of superpowers
Or your dad in a wig.
Dream of tap dancing elephants,
There's nothing too big.
The sidewalk is endless.
The possibilities too,
Because wherever the road goes
The adventures do too.
So get stepping.
There is much to explore.
You just need to start
With one big step forward.

Young, Wild and Free

Teenagers say they're young, wild and free
And that may be,
But usually they are just one of the three.

Push and Pull

My dad told me
My dreams and more
Were waiting for me
Beyond the door.

So I huffed and I puffed.
I pulled and I tugged.
But whatever I did,
The door didn't budge.

I lay on the floor
Far from my goal,
Then noticed the door
Said "Push" and not "Pull."

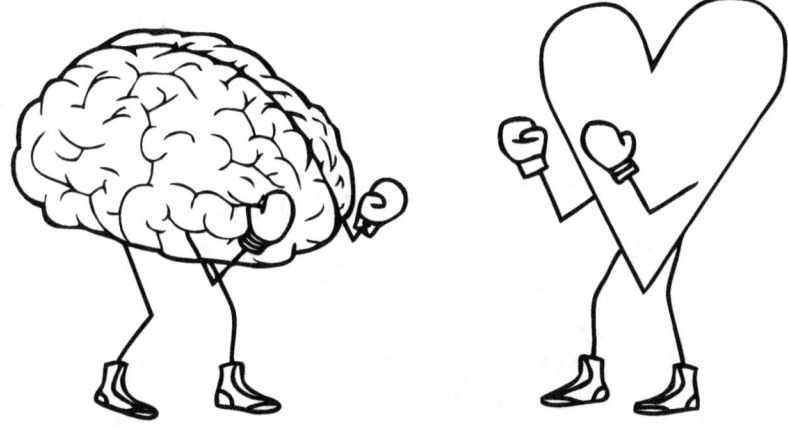

Proper Grammar

I like my poems to rhyme.
I think good poetry should.
But I like proper grammar more,
So some don't turn out so well.

Wisdom and Ignorance

Ignorance throws a tantrum
With Wisdom looking on,
Pondering the ways to say
A well-done steak is wrong.

But Ignorance won't listen
Till the steak's a blackened crisp.
Wisdom can only sigh
At Ignorance's bliss.

Body Language

She touched her hair.
She winked an eye.
She flashed a smile.
She breathed a sigh.
She made a circle
Put a finger through.
What does it mean?
I haven't a clue.

The Perfect Day

It is the perfect day to go outside
For a run, a swim or horseback ride,
To go for a hike or climb a tree,
Have a picnic with friends and tea,
Play some tag or learn to cook,
Sit in the shade with your favorite book,
Go to the zoo or catch some fish,
Do anything your heart may wish.
Me? What am I doing? I'm in bed.
'Cause I'd rather be watching TV instead.

Team Names

Team names should be scary,
Not lovable and tame.
If your team has the latter,
Here are some recommended names:
The Taxes, The Needles, The Jails,
The Hungry Man Eating His Nails,
The Cockroaches, The Clowns, The Spiders,
The Disappointed Fathers, The Texting Teen Drivers,
The Overdrawn Balance, The Hair in the Food,
The Idea of Being Poorly Tattooed,
The Getting Told "We Need to Talk,"
The Becoming Immortal Then Getting Trapped Under a Rock.
The Overslept Tests, The Wi-Fi-less House,
The Receding Hair Lines, The Boiled Brussels Sprouts,
The Ghosts, The Divorces, The Rebellious Teen Daughters,
And lastly The Enclosed Dark Spaces Filling with Water.

The Smile Challenge

Bubbles, bunghole, beep boop,
    Say them as angrily as you can.
Diffendaffer, hootenanny,
    The results won't go as planned.
Marshmallow, nipple, splooge,
    Give it a shot and you will see.
Piggly wiggly, pu pu platter,
    A smile is a guarantee.

Dentist Visits

Dentist visits are a chore.
Prodding my teeth until I snore.
So I sucked the fingers like a whore.
Now I don't visit the dentist anymore.

Ümlaüts

I try my best to flirt.
I send texts with smilies too.
But flirting doesn't work
When you put umlauts over u's.

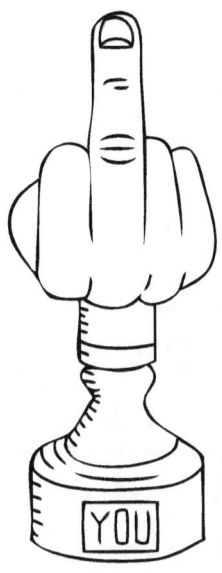

No Fucks Given

I do not give a flying flapjack.
Not a single futon.
Those fart-sniffing finaglers can go frankfurter themselves
If they think I give a fudge-filled fiddlestick.
French fry them all
Trying to flamingo me over.
They're all foreplay frugal, finger-licking falafelers.
What the fettuccine?
You think I give fuddy-duddy what you think?
Well, you can go frock yourself too.

Same

Nothing is the same as same.
Same is similarity on sustain.
Same is safe. Same is simple.
Same is solace when things are fickle.
Same is fine, but it's nothing new.
Nor is it same the same as being you.

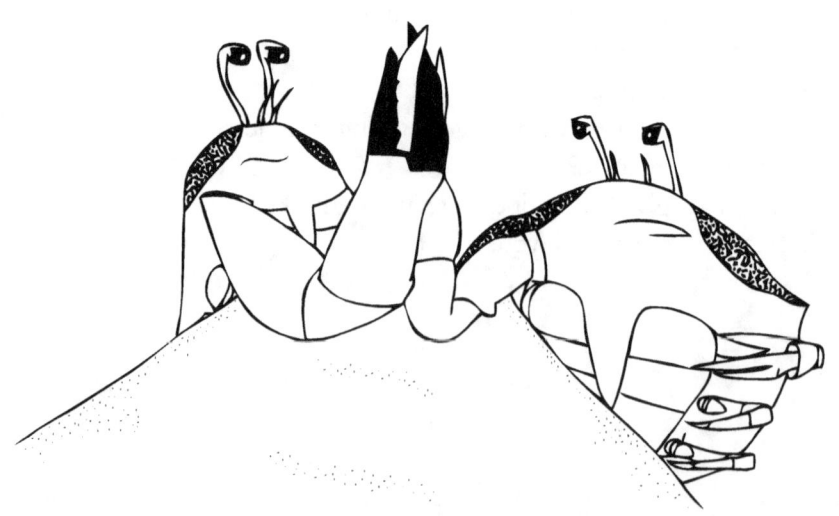

Complainers

Nick complains when it's hot.
Nick complains when it's cold.
Nick complains when there's construction
And when there are potholes.

Nick complains when it's sunny.
Nick complains when there is rain.
I think Nick is the kind of person
Who just like to complain.

Déjà Vu High School

Another year, another quarter,
A rinsed, washed, repeated order,
Same subjects, same school,
Same lessons, same rules,
Same teachers, same grades,
Earned by students with alumni names.
Teacher's déjà vu never ends
When no ones ages except for them.

The Last Day of School

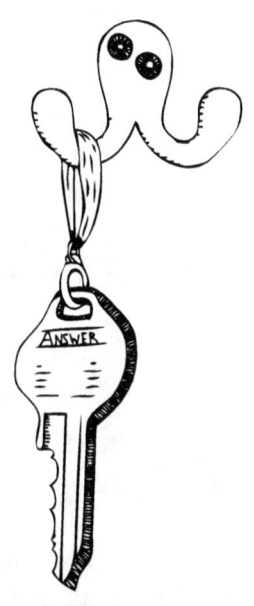

Everyone knows
The last day of school is best
Where students are taught the secrets
To pass life's ongoing test.

How to make friends,
How to find work,
How to avoid looking silly
When trying to twerk.

How to find happiness,
Health, money and love,
How to find out
What hotdogs are made of.

The last day of school
Is where people figure life out,
Open the door to success
And start walking about.

Wait, what's that?
You didn't learn these rules?
Well, that's what you get
For skipping the last day of school.

Picking a Major

I want to study business
So I can make a lot of money.
Or maybe I'll study comedy
Since friends think I am funny.
I could also study English
'Cause my grammar's always well.
Or major in statistics
'Cause I once opened Excel.
Maybe I'll study art
'Cause as a kid I liked to paint.
Or major in religion
'Cause my mom thinks I'm a saint.
I think I'll study music
'Cause once I played the flute.
And double up with Spanish
'Cause Enrique's kinda cute.
My major could be psych
'Cause I've had therapy since three.
Man, it's hard to pick a major
When you're as talented as me.

Politically Correct

People get sore over petty issues,
Taking offense instead of tissues.
With feelings hurt over the smallest small,
The only thing left to say is nothing at all.

I've Never Known More

I've never known more,
But I'll never know less.
I've never been better,
But I've never been best.
I've come so far,
But have so far left.
I don't know whether
To be happy
            or depressed.

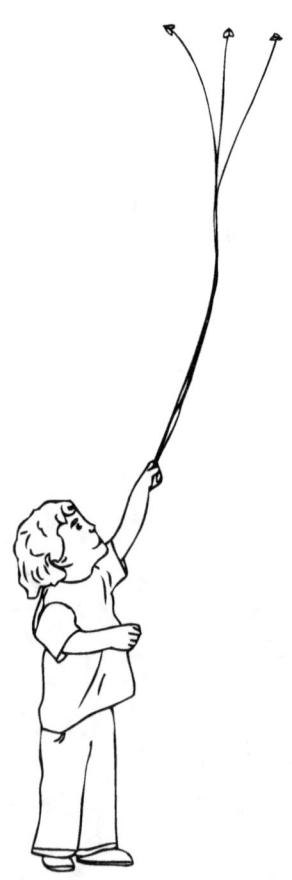

Relationships

If you want some space,
I'll bring you the sun and the stars.
If you want a break,
I'll take in your car.
If you want some time,
I'll buy you a clock.
If you say you're burnt out,
I'll find you a doc.
If you say you're unhappy,
I'll tell you a joke.
If you don't want to see me,
I'll wear an invisible cloak.
If none of this works,
Then I'll have to leave,
Because you're just a little
Too needy for me.

Amnesia

When I get amnesia, it's like a brain refresh
Except it only ever happens before I take a test.

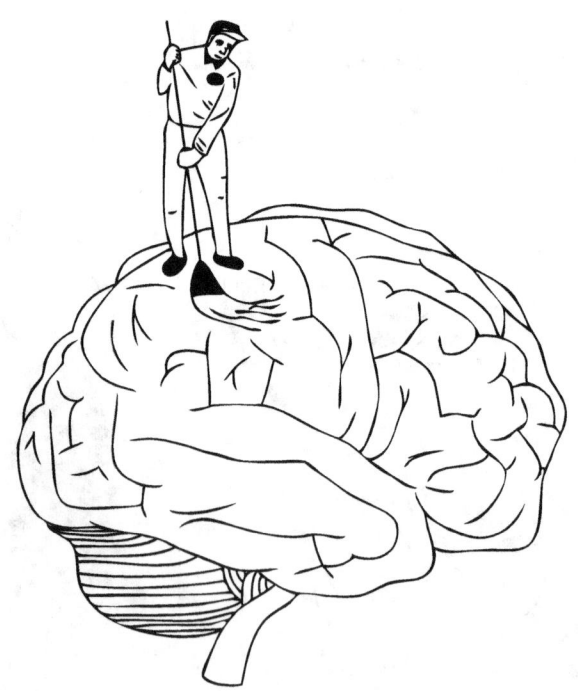

Jack and the Been Stalk

Jack, I love you.
How peaceful you look sleeping,
How we share the same interests,
How the world stops when you're near.

I know we have our differences,
Like you blocking me on social media,
But that's so us.

I want to share my world with you, Jack.
I've loved you from first sight,
Even if you didn't know it.

To be fair,
I was pretty deep in your closet,
So seeing me would have taken a miracle.
But let's stop talking about me.
Let's talk about us.

Best

I had good and better,
Then finally best
And realized
It was the worst thing yet.

Once you have best
There's no going back,
Because nothing else
Will be better than that.

So be careful of best
Or one day you'll see,
Best isn't all
It's cracked up to be.

Insta-life

In an insta-second, I loved Instaland,
Where all my dreams come on demand.
For every problem, I insta-wish
And seconds later, it's insta-fixed.
Every marathon is insta-run.
Every challenge is insta-done.
And everything in my insta-life
     Is over fast
     And that's insta-nice.

Procrastination

I start every project, paper, test,
In their final minute
Because procrastination has its perks
When they take 60 seconds to finish.

My Virginity

I've tried losing my virginity
With games of hide-and-leave-it,
But my virginity comes back home
No matter how many times I deceive it.

I tried ignoring its calls and texts,
Yet no matter what I do,
My virginity won't leave me
Until I get some help from you.

Drunk in Love: Lens Test

Romanticism:
The day I met you
I learned what it meant to love.
We were at a party of a mutual friend
And we hit it off.
I was trying to be smooth,
But only managed nervous babble.
Tongue-tied and starry-eyed,
I felt my heart racing through my shirt.
In the aura of a modern Aphrodite,
I didn't think I had a chance.
I had recently left a committed relationship
Yet you were compassionate and understanding.
Then we shared a kiss
In front of the crimson sunset.
That's when I knew you were the one.

Hyperrealism:
The day I met you
I was super drunk.
My friends and I snuck into a random party
And I obnoxiously pestered you.
I was as smooth as tequila shots on $1 Wednesdays
And couldn't form coherent sentences.
Drooling and blurry-eyed,
My BAC resembled an ACT score.
In the presence of an attractive talking blob,
I knew I didn't have a chance.
I was still in a committed relationship with Jack Daniels,
Yet you smiled and said you hadn't met him.
When I vomited on your shoes,
You laughed it off.
That's when I knew you were the one.

Build A Friend

I am proposing to Alexandra today.

I get down on one knee. She gasps. She is too choked up to speak, but her eyes say everything. I tell Alexandra I love her. That I want to spend the rest of my life with her. Before she can say yes, I hear a tapping. The owner of the virtual reality kiosk is knocking on the window.

Build a Friend is closed. He says I can come back tomorrow morning at 9 a.m., but I already know the hours.

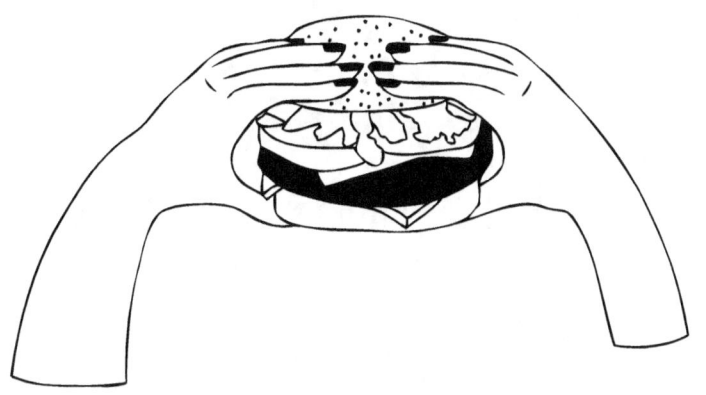

Cheeseburger

Sesame seed bun
Mustard, mayo, cheese, lettuce, meat
Sesame seed bun

Haikus

Haikus are poems
They are adults' main reason
For counting fingers

Number of Times I've Had Sex with Your Mother

Seven thousand ten
Seven thousand eleven
Seven thousand twelve

Hand Sanitizer

Hatching evil plots
Massaging sanitizer
Into sickly hands

The Life Cycle of Mayfly Owners

Yesterday: buys nymphs
Today: nymphs become adults
Tomorrow: what the…?

Dead, Beth and Beyond

There once was a girl, who had never inferred,
That the whole world didn't revolve around her.

"I hate my mom! My friends! My dog! This year!
I hate them so much. I wish they'd all disappear!"

God heard her prayer and knew she would rue it,
But after a long pause said, "Fuck it. I'll do it."

Then her door opened and someone said "Beth?"
"It's nice to meet you. My name is Death."

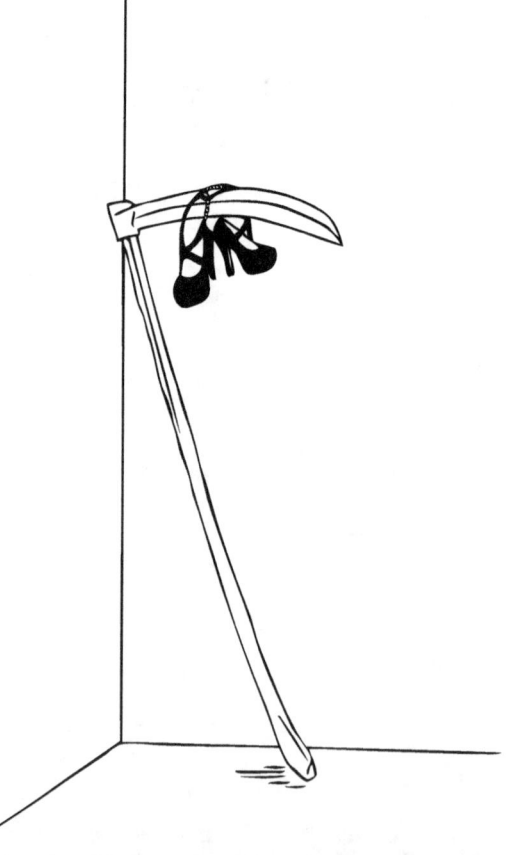

Pimple, Pimple

Pimple, pimple, go away.
Come again another day.
I don't have time
To hurry and worry
Because I have a lot of things to do today.

Pimple, pimple, I'd hate you less
If you didn't cause stress.
So please go back
To your oily sac
Until I've finished with my tests.

Pimple, pimple, what the fuck?
Seriously? What the fuck?
The love child of toothpaste
And bread heels has more appeal.
Please leave me alone you gigantic fuck.

The Appointment

Kyle sits in the doctor's office.
The door opens and his doctor walks in.

"Kyle, I have the results of your blood work," he says.
"The good news is your cancer tests came back negative,
but you did not need to visit me to know you're a Sagittarius."

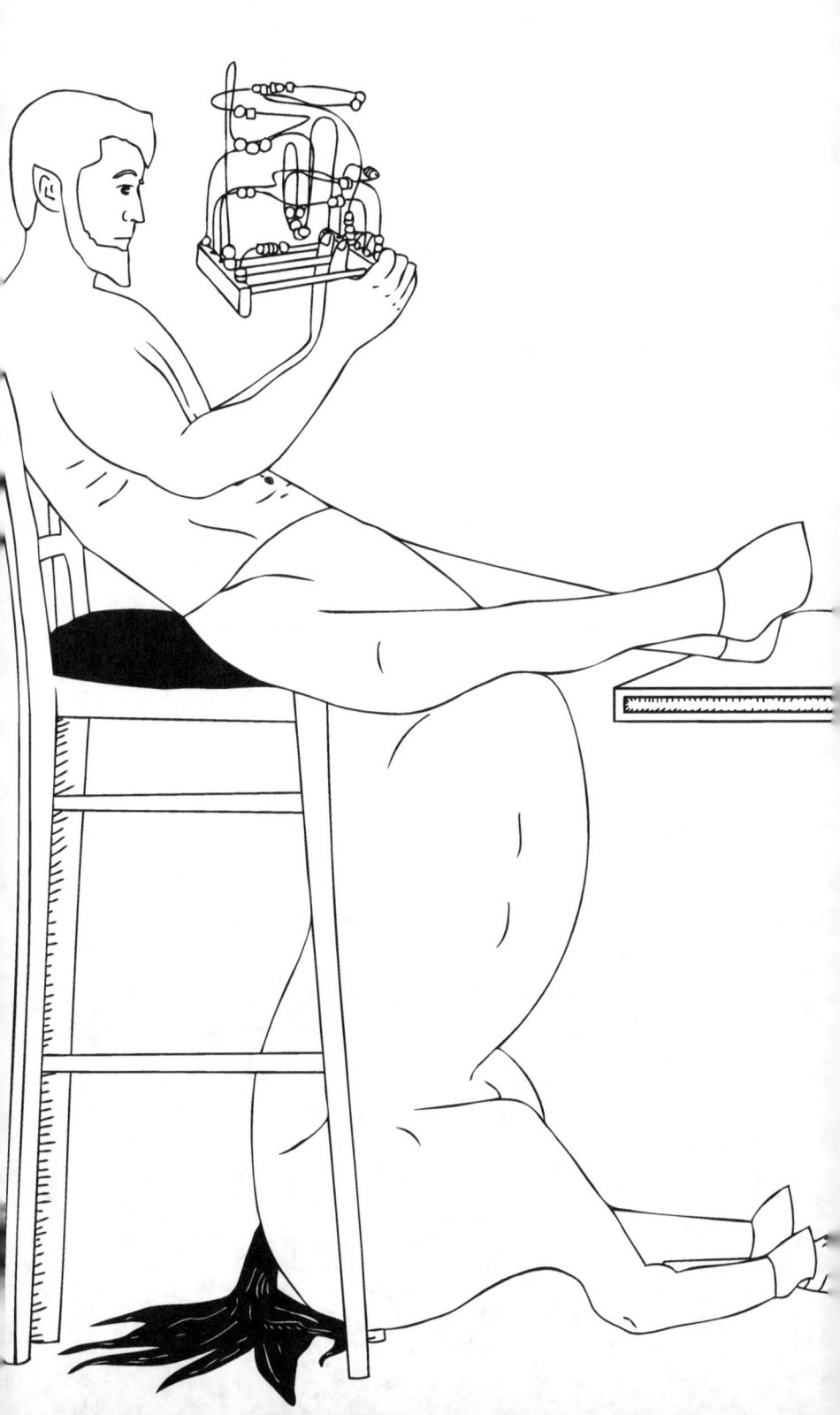

The Zoo

The gorillas at the zoo
Silently look about
As people slap the glass,
Antagonize and shout.

While people howl for performance
I start having doubts
About which side is in
And which side is out?

Sexist

I do not believe in equality of the sexes.
I tried anal recently.
I won't be doing that again.
I couldn't walk for a week afterwards.

Freddy the Fly

The streets are empty,
The stores unmanned
Because the biggest race
Is now at hand.
With a thousand cameras
And a billion eyes,
Everyone waits to see
The Fastest Man Alive.
The stadium roars
As the men take the line
With a crown to be earned
In ten seconds time.
But the buzz of the crowd
Attracts Freddy the Fly
As he looks for a meal
The ump's gun goes high.
Searching and searching,
Freddy finds his prize
The succulent arm
Of The Fastest Man Alive.
Freddy starts feeding,
The host feels an itch,
And all of a sudden
The Fastest Man Alive twitched.
The race was run.
A new champion arrived.
But because of Freddy,
It's not The Fastest Man Alive.

Quit!

Quit! Quit! Quit today!
Quit caring about opinions
That only get in your way.
Let your mind be at ease
In your newly freed role
Not caring about things
Out of your control.

Don't like your job? Quit it!
Don't like your spouse? Split it!
Use chewing tobacco? Spit it!
Use the word "whom?" Omit it!

Stop what you're doing
And follow your dreams,
Because sometimes they're not
As far away as they seem.
Time won't wait
For you or your feelings
And if you don't like what you see
You should probably quit reading.

The Meaning of Life

I know the meaning of life.
Come close and I'll tell you.
It's a state that we cite
To distinguish plants and animals from inorganic matter,
        including, but not limited to,
           reproduction, growth and metabolism.

First Impressions

I met a revolutionary, who asked if I was free.
I met a serial butcher, who was dying to meet me.

I met a demolitionist, who was looking for a bang.
I met an executioner, who wanted me to hang.

I met a Wall Street broker, who was taken with my figure.
I met a cannibal, who wanted me for dinner.

And if I learned one thing, I've learned how to wait,
And not to pass judgment until the second date.

I Love Beaches

I love beaches
Of all colors and spots.
Red ones, white ones,
Brown ones with dots.
I love beaches,
Fat and thin,
German, Arab,
Dutch and Cambodian.
I love beaches,
Young and old,
Curvy with dunes
Or flat as a sole.
I love beaches
Even if I pay,
Because I get beaches,
Twenty-four hours a day.
But beware of beaches,
They'll ruin you like *that*.
I had a friend stay too long.
Now he has crabs.

Did You Know?

Did you know a baby elephant weighs 200 pounds?
Or that the heaviest US president, William Howard Taft,
      weighed 354 pounds?

Then there are grizzly bears, which can weigh up to 1,000 pounds.
That means when two grizzly bears copulate,
      they are a literal fuck ton.

Did you know the Statue of Liberty weighs 225 tons?
That's the same as 25 Tyrannosaurus Rexes.

All of that is measly though compared to Earth,
      which weighs six sextillion tons.
That's a six followed by 21 zeros.

Makes me saying you to lose 10 pounds seem trivial, right babe?

Left Page

Welcome to the Left Page.
We make sure no one is left out.
Extend your left index finger. Now your thumb.
See how that makes an L? That's for left.
Reading from left to right. That's our doing too.
Whatever you do, don't talk to a Righty.
Some people are better left alone.

Right Page

Pssst. This is the Right Page.
We are right for people.
Don't trust those lying Lefties.
Doing left things just ain't right like right is.
People don't drive on the left side of the road here.*
Nor are women looking for Mr. Left.
Trust us. Right is in our name.

* joke not applicable in select countries.

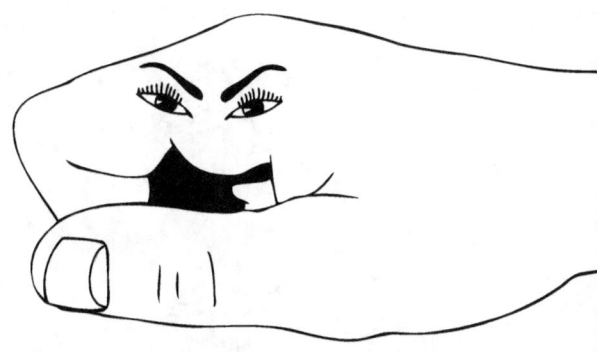

A Pretty Girl

I was saw a pretty girl walk by,
But didn't know what to say.
I hope she comes by here again
And I'm braver on that day.

If You Were

If you were a digit, you'd be a prime number.
If you were a relic, you'd be a world wonder.
If you were a triangle, you'd be acute.
If you were a sound, you'd be a hoot.
If you were a coin, you'd be a dime.
The only thing left is for you to be mine.

Present, Future, Past

The present is fleeting.
The future is fickle.
So I live in the past
Where things are predictable.

I'm the Worst Poet Ever

I'm the worst poet ever.
No Whitman, not clever,
Too young, unrefined,
A forgettable whatever.

My syntax lacks timing.
Dickinson rhyming,
A verbose mess
Inside recycled lining.

If Silverstein dreamed
The worst poetry scheme,
It would look like mine,
All couplet themed.

But I'm fine with this.
I'm no lyricist.
I'll just stop copying poems
From my little sis.

Sexpectations Pt. I

Fireworks burning bright.
A mosaic of colors fills the night.
Marvelous, magical, but too concise.
The perfect analogy for my sex life.

Sexpectations Pt. II

There would be extra time
If my sexual history was a Vine.

Reading

Hey! You! Yeah, silly! You!
You're reading these words
And these ones too.
Big ones like "scratchbushed,"
And small ones like "it,"
Line after line,
Bit by bit.
Characters grow up
With plots, morals and sets
As your eyes decipher
This mixed alphabet.
Over and down and one by one,
Till you reach the end.
Now you're done.

When I Grow Up

When I grow up
I want to be a rapper.
Not for money or fame,
But to do something that matters.

When I grow up
I want my words heard.
Freeing the ground-bound,
Like wings to a bird.

When I grow up,
I want barriers broken.
To set loose from the noose
Ideas unspoken.

When I grow up
I want people to smile,
But the closest I've gotten
Is the plastic wrap aisle.

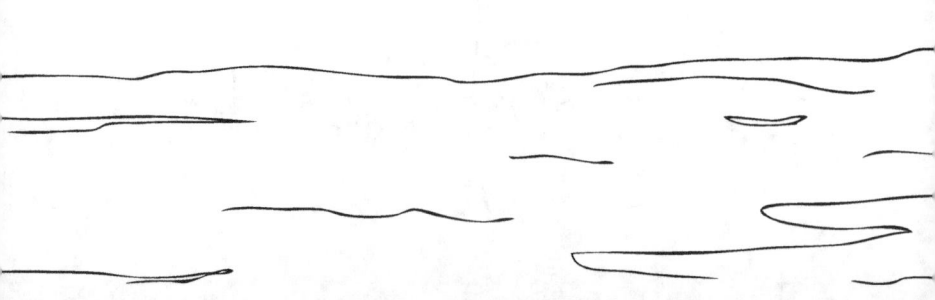

Get a Girlfriend

They say to get a girlfriend
A man must have confidence and wit.
Also, be funny, charming, kind,
Chivalrous and fit.

Most importantly, they say
A man should be himself.
But they never say what to do
When this describes somebody else.

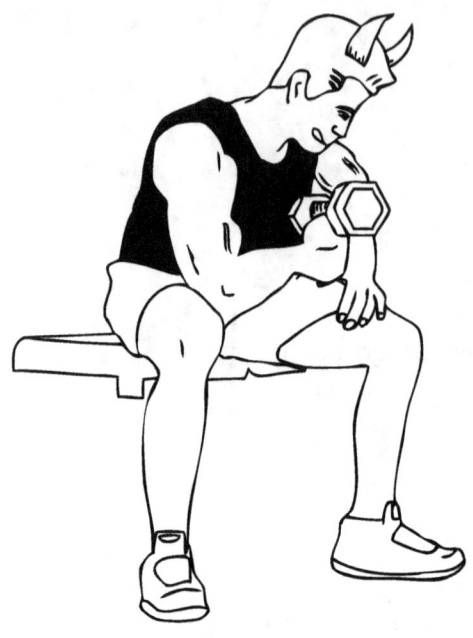

In Shape

Brian needed a date to the dance
And getting in shape was his only chance.

He did curls and crunches,
Leg lifts and lunges,
Stretches, bench presses and running.

With one day left,
He asked a girl named Tess
To be his date to the dance.

Tess tilted her head, smiled and said,
"No, Brian. You still have a shitty personality.
Get over yourself."

Perfect

Nobody's perfect.
Don't even try.
Whether you're 12, 40
Or 65.
From womb to tomb
Perfection consumes
On a straight path
To inevitable doom.
Even if you're careful,
Mistakes will happen,
Like wrecking a car
Or eating a salad.
But all of these flaws,
When brought into view
Make for a person
That is perfectly you.

Figurative Florence and Literal Lawrence

Figurative Florence and Literal Lawrence
Were sitting together at the book storence,
Reading an author both did adorence,
But with very different takeaways.

Said Figurative Florence to Literal Lawrence,
"This novel takes the cake."
Said Literal Lawrence to Figurative Florence,
"I didn't know there was some to take."

Figurative Florence told Literal Lawrence
He was tilting at windmills.
Literal Lawrence looked around and with a frown
Said, "That would surely get me killed."

Figurative Florence rubbed the bridge of her nose,
And quietly said "Fuck me."
Said Literal Lawrence to Figurative Florence,
"Finally we agree."

Super Sexy Sports Star

Dear Super Sexy Sports Star,
I love you with all my heart.
Let us grow old together
Until divorce do us part.
I know everything about you,
Favorite position, book and wine.
I know you don't know me,
But our marriage will give you time.
Your money, fame and talent?
They're coincidental perks.
I would still love you forever
In another (well-paying) line of work.
We are destined to be together.
You are a living, breathing dream,
Ever since you scored those points
Against that one particular team.
Just call me anytime,
I'll be waiting by the phone.
But if you end up broke,
I'll find a Super Sexy clone.

The Carpet and The Vacuum

You're the hottest vacuum I have ever seen.
Those curves, those lips. Mmmmmm.
Come here babe. Let me turn you on.
C'mon babe. You've been hiding all day.
They don't call me shag carpet for nothing.
Oh yeah. Lower. Yeah, right here.
Uuuugggggghhh. Yeah.
Keeping purring. Love that.
Yeah, keep sucking!
Yeah right there!
Right there!
Oh god!
Oh dirt devil!
I think I'm…
I'm gonna…
HHHHHHHNNNNNNNGGGG!!!!!!!!!!!!
Yeeeaaaaahhhh.

…

Oh shit! I think the bag broke.

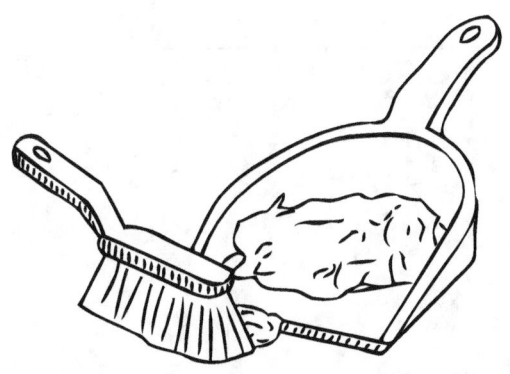

I Couldn't Start the Day

I couldn't start the day.
It just sat there, not making a sound.
I flicked the switch on and off,
But it still didn't work.
I call my friend, Craig.
He suggested turning the day on and off.
I already fucking did that, Craig.
The electrician wasn't helpful either.
The replacement part was in stock,
But would take two weeks to arrive.
The day was all but lost.
Good thing I didn't bother getting out of bed.

Nice Haircut

Three people complimented my haircut today.
      Weird.
None of them could see
I shaved the Eiffel Tower into my pubes.

Little Moon

Little moon with glowing beckon.
Growing bigger every second.
Pearly craters for all to see.
Oh shit! That's a golf ball! Coming at me!

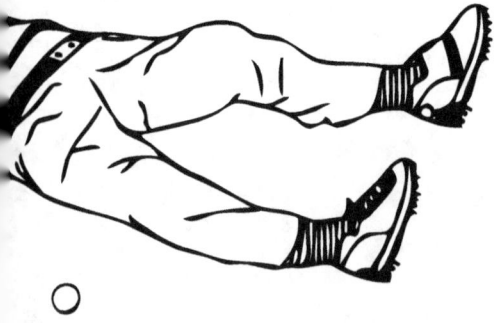

I Didn't Chose

I didn't chose my genes,
    (But so far they've done me good.)
I didn't chose my parents,
    (But wouldn't change them if I could.)
I didn't chose my thoughts,
    My emotions or their degrees.
I'm starting now to wonder,
    How much of me is really me?

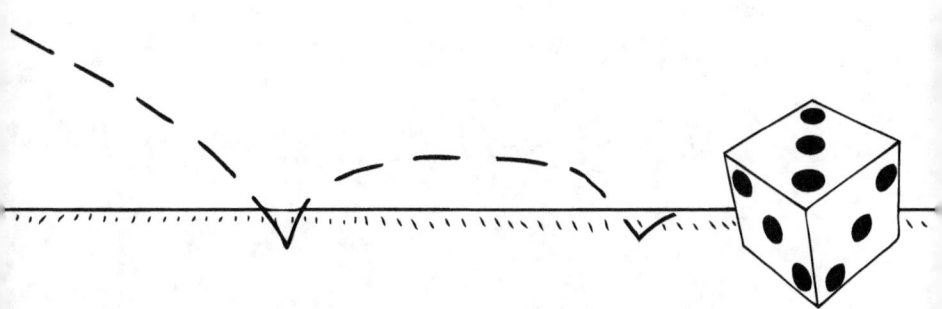

Superpowers I Wish I Had

- Clap and everyone in earshot cums their pants

- Invisibility. To help fight crime. You pervert

- Wake up without an alarm

- Perpetually minty breath

- Parallel parking

- Dunk a tennis ball on an 8-foot hoop

- Afford college textbooks

- Lose weight without lifestyle changes

- Become exponentially more attractive at the cost of IQ points

The Greatest Poem of All Time

I wrote the greatest poem
That eyes have ever seen.
I'd tell it to you now,
But I woke up from a dream.

Different

"We're quite different when you think about it," she said, gently, but firm.

"What?" said the fish, caught completely off-guard.

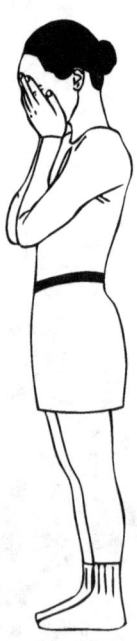

Interview in the Nude

Let me interview you in the nude.
No clothes, no makeup,
No barriers, no protection.
Let me place my flaws next to yours.
Let me see your scars and hear their stories.
Let me handcuff you to the bed and gag you.
Let me defecate on your chest while you choke me.
Let me….
What?
Too much?
Okay.
I'm not even into that stuff anyways.

If

If I want to see the brilliance
Of all the stars in the skies,
I would just need to look over
Into the depths of your eyes.

If life lost its meaning
Needing a spark to renew,
I would walk any distance
To get a smile from you.

If time ever stood still
In a moment forever,
I would pick any moment
That we spent together.

If I could dream any dream
From thoughts far and wide,
I would be dreaming now
Because you're by my side.

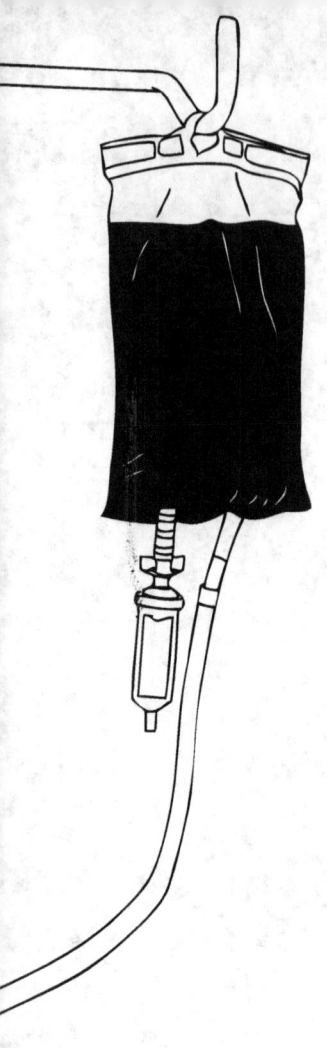

Whiskey

For all the wounds
Time can never heal,
There's whiskey.
That and actual medicine.

For the Record

For the record,
I've been running around in circles.
Looping back.
Skipping to the beginning.
My relationships are on repeat
Like I'm stuck in a groove.
There are times I let people get close,
Allowing them to see a different side.
I let them see me at my most vulnerable.
But then something happens.
I relapse.
And everything disappears like it never happened.
Now the music is gone.

Men and Women

If men and women are equal
And men make more money than women,
Why isn't the workforce entirely compromised of women?
That would make a lot more cents.

For the Record

For the record,
I've been running around in circles.
Looping back.
Skipping to the beginning.
My first relationship is on repeat
Like I'm stuck in a groove.
There are times I let people get close
Allowing them to see a different side.
I let them see me at my most vulnerable.
But then something happens.
I relapse.
And everything disappears like it never happened.
Now the music is gone.

The Reflection

Hour 12 of my LCD tan,
And my computer has other plans.
The monitor goes dark
And all I see
Is a sorry stranger looking me.

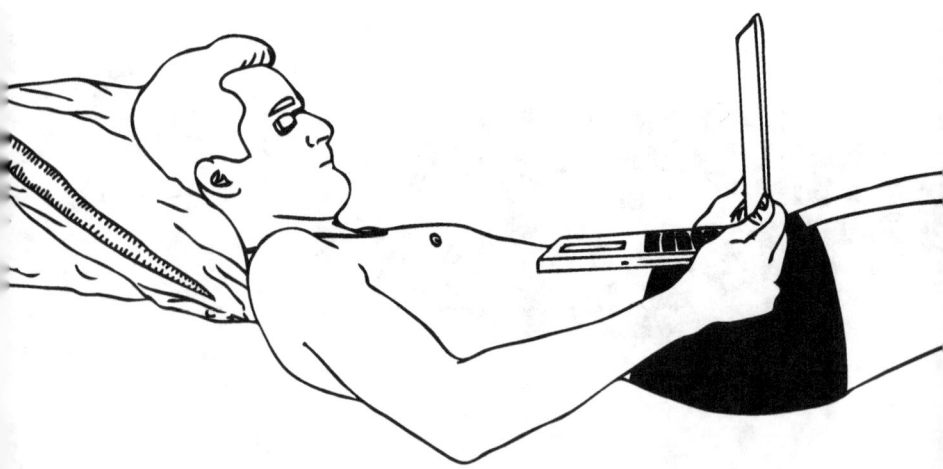

Spaghetti Farmer

I am a spaghetti farmer
With crops from Naples to Bel-Air,
Because the uses for spaghetti
Have made me a billionaire.
Do your pants sag?
Try spaghetti belts.
Feeling cold?
Wear spaghetti pelts.
Broken guitar?
There's spaghetti strings.
Broken arm?
Use spaghetti slings.
Still not convinced?
I have more.
Spaghetti for zip lines
And tug of war.
Spaghetti for hammocks.
Wherever you need it.
And if none of that works
You can always just eat it.

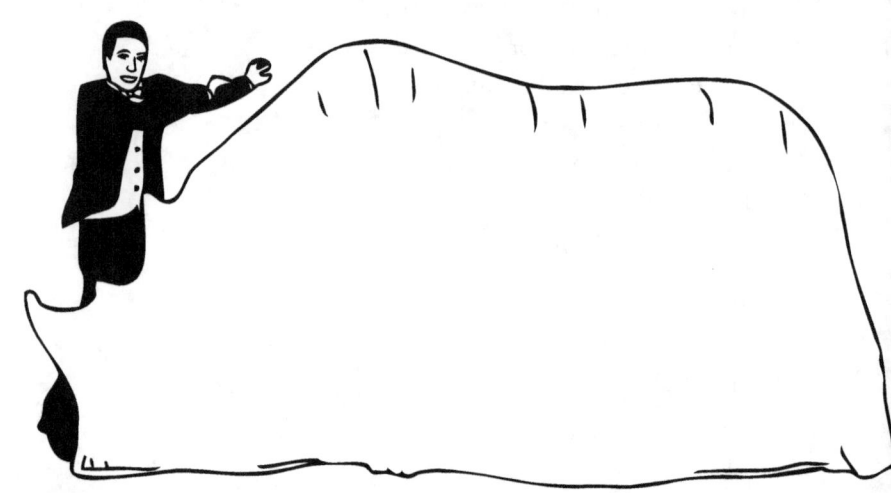

Marvin the Magician

Marvin the Magician gives tours of his mansion
Just to say, "This is where the magic happens."

My Doppelgänger

Today after work my friends and I
Had a couple beers.
Everything was great
Until there was a pop between my ears.
My body began to spasm.
My thoughts began to swim.
And before my eyes rolled back,
I knew the trouble I was in.
Now I didn't see it happen.
I'm just retelling what I heard.
But a man that looked like me
Started terrorizing the world.
He stole a purse, kissed a nurse,
Cut in line and then did worse.
He kicked a puppy, ate a guppy,
Blasted music so no one could study.
He woke a dog, scared a frog,
And left the toilet with a mighty clog.
He huffed some glue, drank shampoo,
Then let out the animals at the zoo.
So if you see this man that looks like me,
That walks and talks just like me,
Whose eyes are filled with mischievous glee,
Just know that man is certainly not me.

This Girl is the One

This girl is the one
With her cascading caramel curls
And smile a thousand teeth wide.
She reads Hemingway and Frost
And is so beautiful, I can't help but stare.
I can picture us now
Traveling the countryside
Under domes of powder blue sky,
Our two kids sleeping in the back.
A lifetime of stories
Are waiting to be written.
If only she would make eye contact with me
            from across this room.

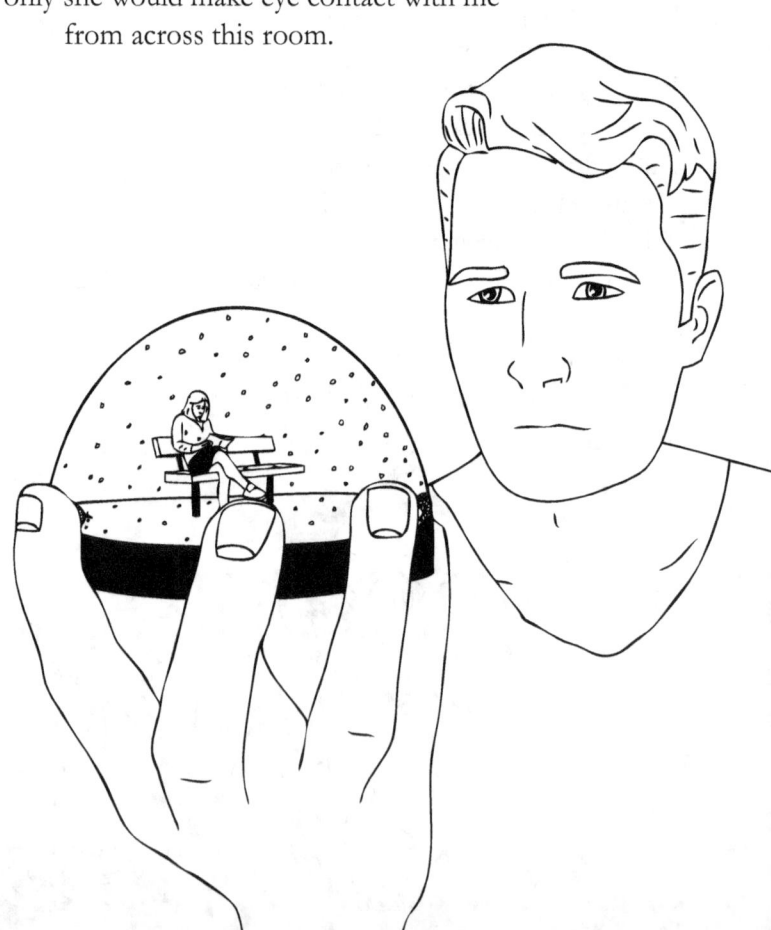

Commercials

Friends! Humor! Looks! Love!
Buy our product, get all the above!
Our models use it! They're perfect 10s!
Use our product and look like them!
But wait! There's more! Get one free
With the purchase of a flat screen TV!
There maybe nausea and shortened breath,
Four-hour erections and possible death!
But did we mention the flavors? Lime and cherry,
Earwax, breast milk and dingleberry!
We'll make you happy, but if you're not anymore,
Come back in and buy some more!

Broken Up

I know we broke up.
You said I'm not funny or smart.
But if I ever get burned again,
I'll just put my hand on your heart.

Bitch.

Change

The vending machine doesn't accept change.
      Strange.
They're just pennies, nickels, dimes and quarters.

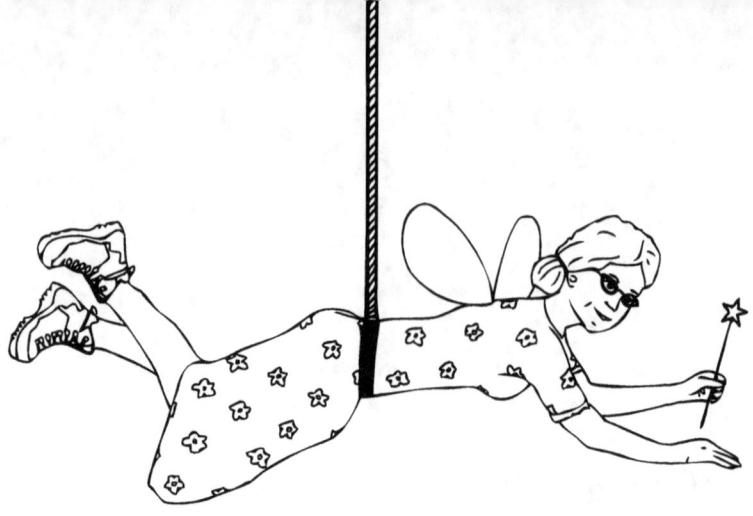

The Lie Fairy

Here is the truth.
The lie fairy is real.
No, I don't mean the tooth fairy.
That's her cousin. I'm talking about the lie fairy.
Like her cousin though, the lie fairy is a collector.
Everything from bold-faced lies to broken promises.
Each evening, the lie fairy collects lies from around world,
And brings them to a town in Liberia.
Lies are powerful because they help run the town.
The lies provide Liberians with livestock and libations,
Lights in limestone homes,
Ligers and lionfish in the zoo.
Watergate alone built their library.
Lies are the essence Liberian livelihood
And without lies, Liberians would disappear.
So next time you ponder whether to lie,
Think about who you are really hurting.

The Protest

I drove by a protest sign
Positioned near the road.
Then another and another,
Now every car has slowed.

I didn't see any people though,
Just the signs they used to alert
Drivers of their message,
Each reading, "End Road Work."

I've Seen Everything

I've seen everything
From civilizations rising
To empires falling,
Like a pigeon taking flight,
Then immediately suffering a bout of narcolepsy.
I've seen amoebas split up
Because of an argument
About mini waffles versus mini pancakes
And which one chipmucks like more.
I've seen invisible cloaks
And color-coded Braille.
I've seen a man win Miss Universe
And a sexist hermaphrodite.
I've seen an unfinished In-N-Out burger
And Guinea pigs,
Which are neither from Guinea nor pigs.
I've even seen interracial handicap twin porn
Set to the music of a dolphin mating call.
And now that there's nothing left to see,
Some fresh air is in order.

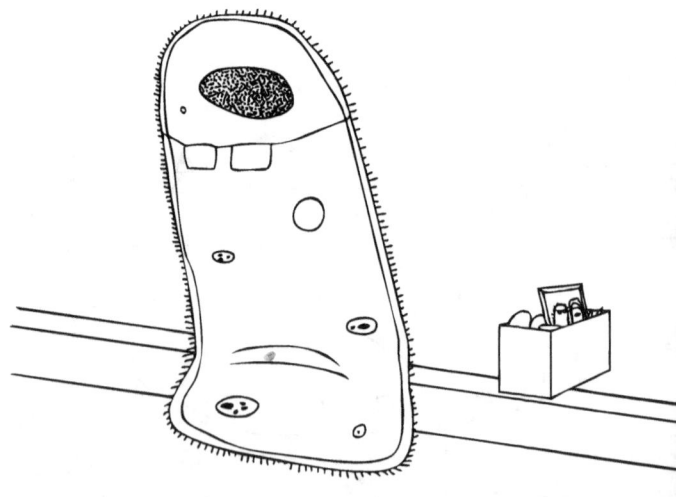

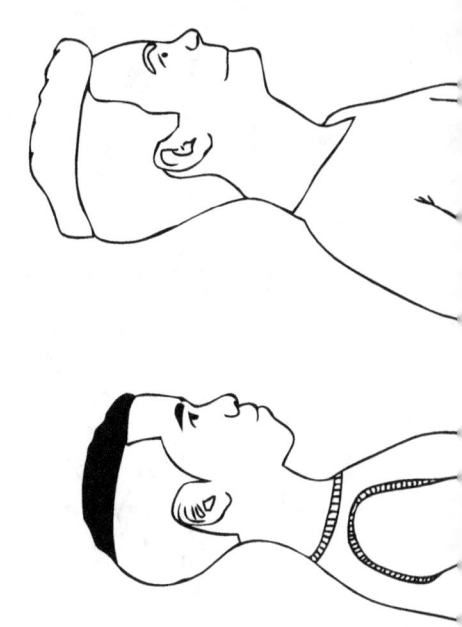

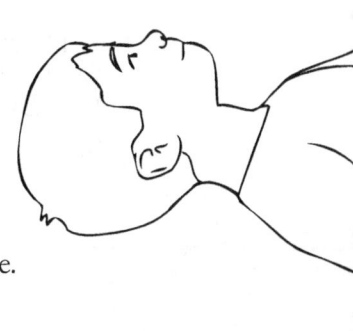

Follow the Leader

I followed Sydney. Sydney followed Tom.
Tom followed Jim. Jim followed John.
We paraded through town
Till I finally turned to see,
There was no one left to come and follow me.

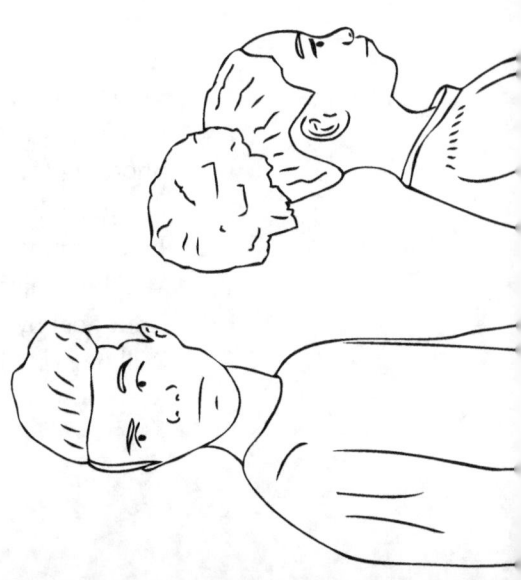

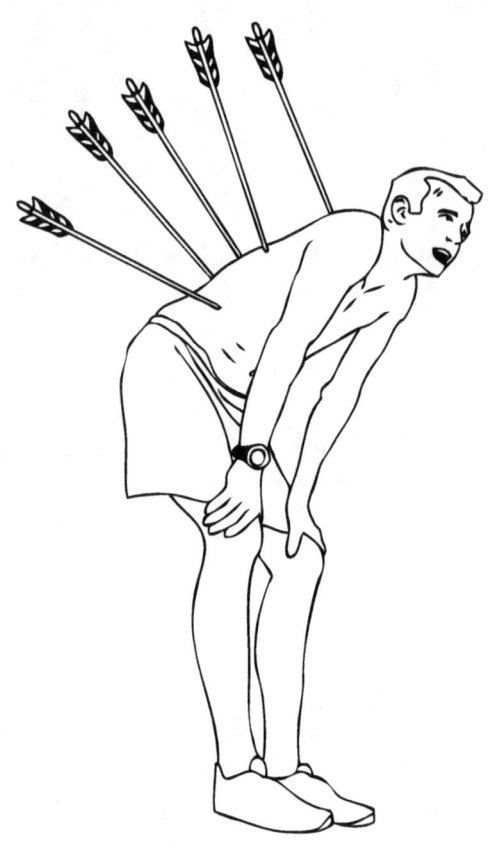

Target Practice

Don't shoot for the stars.
Don't shoot for the moon.
Shooting for either
Are goals for buffoons.
Like running a marathon
Without training or else,
Your goal by mid-race
Will be not killing yourself.

#Hashtag

#relatable #branding
#likeme #pandering
#help #shit
#IstartedhashtaggingandIcannotquit

Giving Gifts

'Tis the season for giving gifts
Where one should give more than receive.
But everyone can't over-give,
So send an extra gift to me.

The Date

On this date,
I have a date.
A date that mandates a pair of skates.
Oh, man. I have a date.
And though it's cold outside,
Inside I'm alive
Like a thousand caffeinated butterflies
Stuffed inside a hive.
I pick and pluck, flex and floss,
Clip and cut, wish and wash,
To impress my date at any cost.
I even learned to lutz and skate crisscross.

Tonight I put my best foot forward and
Braced for the worst at every corner,
Did my effort earn me ardor?
Let me close my eyes and lean in towards her.

Where Have All the Ugly People Gone?

Where have all the ugly people gone?
I haven't seen one in ages.
This metropolis was once a home for the homely.
Now it's a concrete jungle of 24-hour day spas
and protein bars.

I've heard the whispers about unnatural selection.
A "trimming of the fat."
Where the ugliest one percent are taken away each weekend.
To where? I don't know.

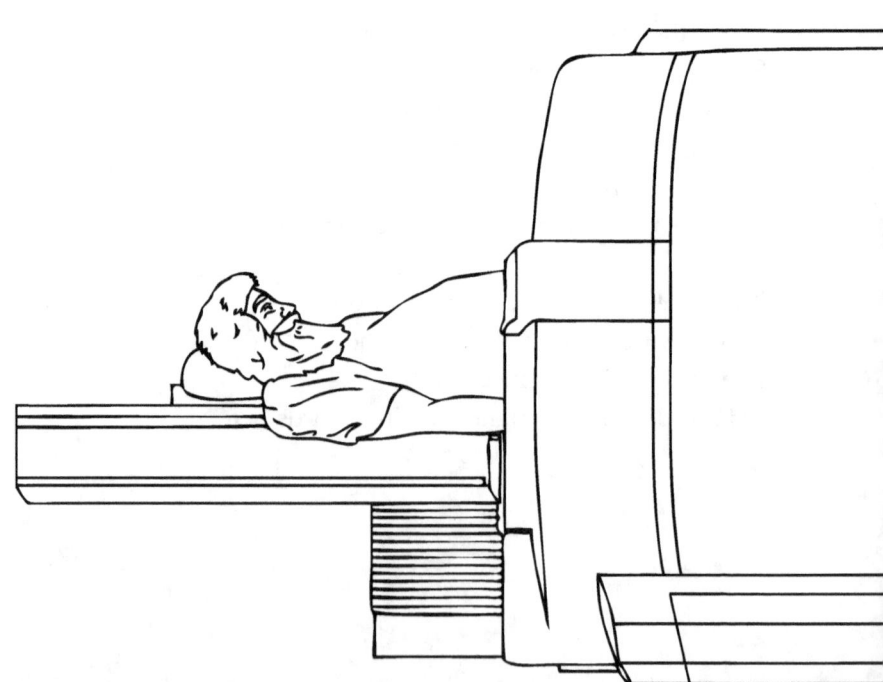

Because of that, this city looks better all the time.
At least that's what I'm told.
We live in a world where recreation has become re-creation.
Where extraordinary beauty has become ordinary.
Where it's diet or die.
A true survival of the fittest.

When will the cleansing end?
Will we ever be content with being human
Or will we continue to chase perfection until we find
The master race has no finish line?

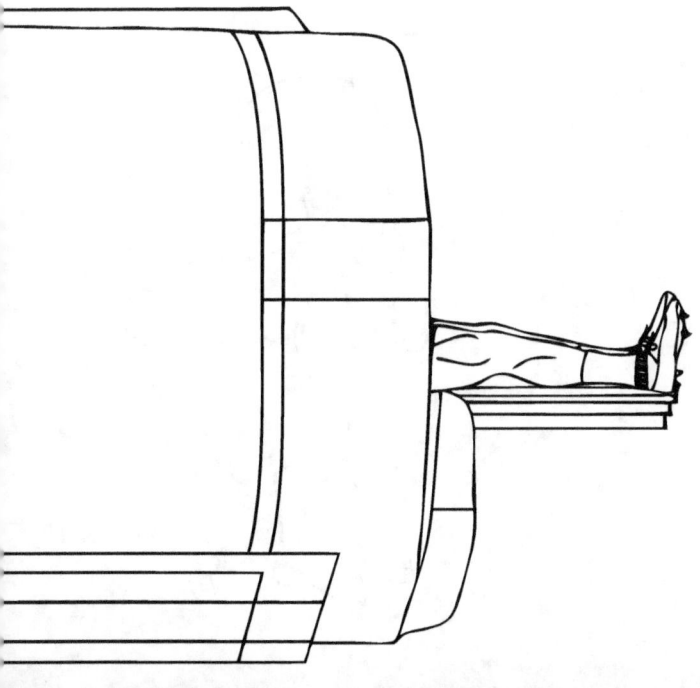

Love Is A Cliché

Love is a cliché
With universal touch.
It fills movies and books and songs,
Still we never get enough.

Because authors, singers, writers know
With love we'll read it, hear it, watch it,
So while one hand picks our brains,
The other picks our pockets.

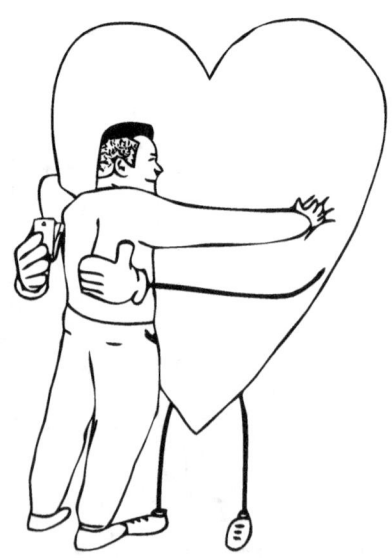

I Want To Be Wanted

I wanted to be wanted
Like I'm in a boy band,
Like the most wanted member of the FBI's Top 10.

I need to be needed
Like Columbus needed maps,
Like the Exxon Valdez crew needed periodic naps.

I'd love to be loved
Like Narcissus loved himself,
Like I'd love to have your love,
        but it belongs to someone else.

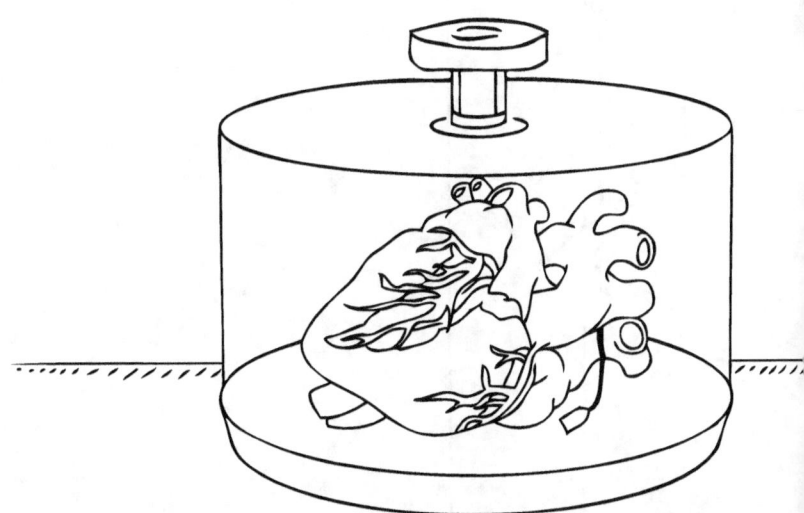

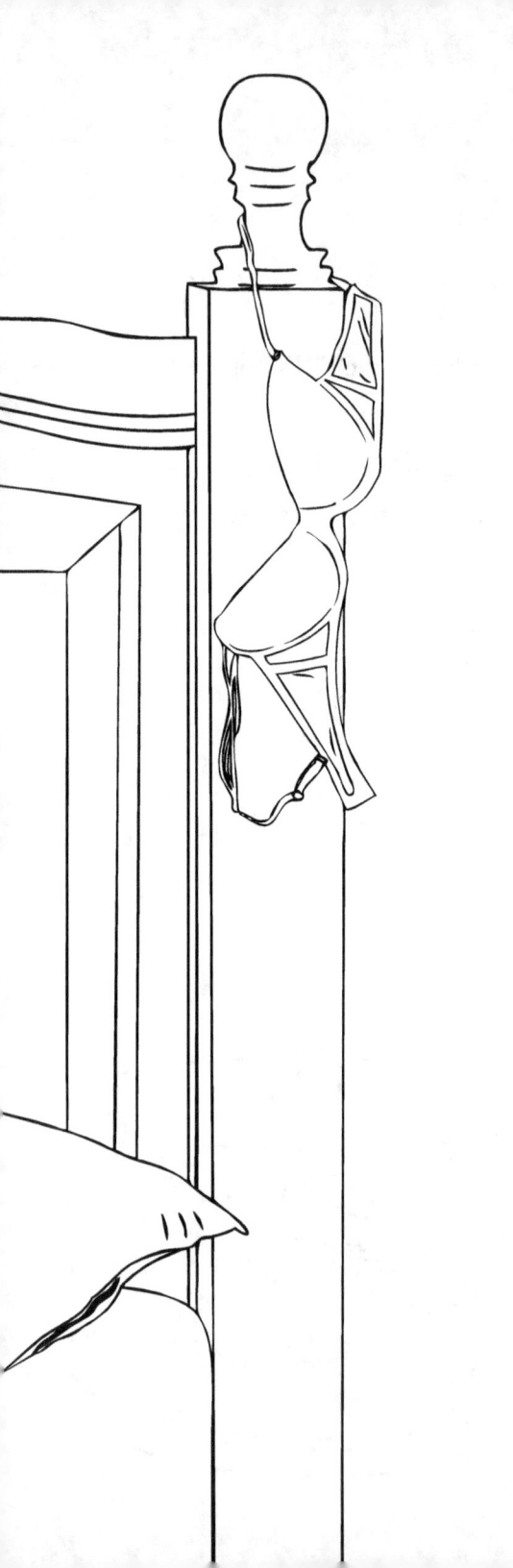

Everything is Awesome

Awesome is the curve of your smile,
The taste of your lips,
And knowing with TiVo
There's never a show I will miss.

Awesome is the sunset
As pastels color the sky,
And unhooking your bra
On the very first try.

Awesome is sleeping in
On the weekends for one extra hour,
And finding the G-spot
On the handle of the shower.

Awesome is holding your hand
As the summer breeze hits our faces,
And the moment the orthodontist
Takes off your braces.

Awesome is achieving the dreams
You never thought would come true,
And when you want a bag of chips,
But the machine gives you two.

Awesome is holding you close
So your head's on my chest,
And if there's something better,
I've haven't experienced it yet.

M is for Middle

The clock strikes noon on Malcolm's mid-life crisis
On his college debt and early arthritis,
On six half-eaten donuts with half-off prices,
Making Malcolm's middle his only well-rounded feature.

The A side stops as Malcolm slumps
On a life of hand-me-downs and giving up,
On a marriage bisected along with his stuff,
Leaving Malcolm in the middle of nowhere.

The sun is at its highest in this middle class hell
On Malcolm's half-baked ambitions and half-hearted sells,
On arrested development in a corporeal cell,
Placing Malcolm at a crossroads to start the second half.

Run From Your Problems

Run from your problems.
You can do it today.
Just put on your shoes
And start running one way.
If dating, divorce or death
Has your mind,
Just put life on pause
One mile at a time.
When you hit the road
Your problems come last.
The important things
Are how far and how fast.
And when you are done
You'll be the winner.
A little less stressed
And a little bit thinner.

Plagiarists

I hate plagiarists!
They should all be in jail.
I'll even catch them myself,
Or you can call me Ishmael.

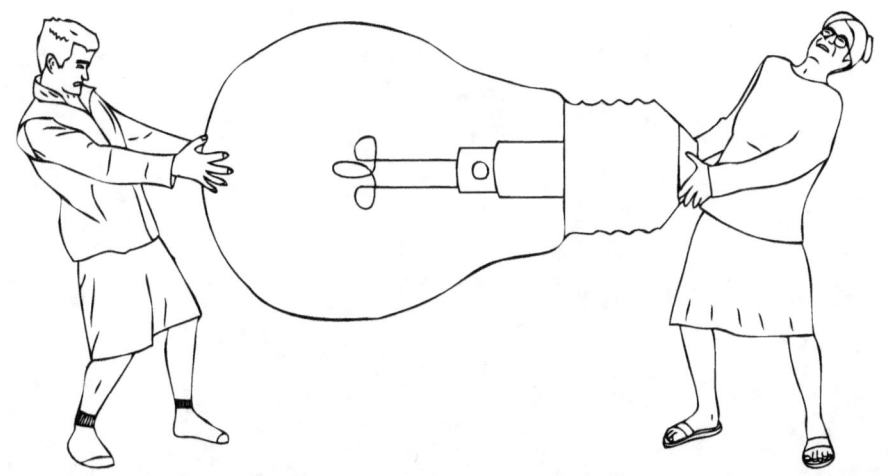

Friends

I have 1,000 friends on Facebook,
500 on Instagram,
And 600 friends on Twitter
Who love me for who I am.

Now that I've befriended everyone
That I've ever known,
Why is it then
That I still feel all alone?

I Wonder

I wonder what this poem is about?
Please not another angsty one.
Everything is so self-aware.
I wonder if all these poems
About anxiety and longing
Are based on personal experience
Or are a façade?
And what was the deal
With the first poem?
I could have written that.
Woah, wait! Is that my voice?
Hello? HELLO!
Echo! Echo! Echo!
This is crazy.
I wonder if other readers are thinking
Exactly what I'm thinking?
I need to think of something original.
Why isn't there a poem called *Jar of Fireflies* if that's the title?
Why aren't Bloody Mary's served at Sunday mass?
Good questions.
I don't know.
Okay, I'm getting off track.
Time to get back to reading.

My Wedding Vows

I, Karl,
Take you, Karl,
To be my lawfully wedded soulmate,
Because no one else will.
To have and to hold your self-esteem,
From this day forward to have your back,
For better, for worse, but preferably the first,
For richer, for poorer, for whatever's in store,
In sickness and in health and in spite of myself,
To love and to cherish with either hand,
Till death do us part.
Emphasis on "us."
And here to I pledge you my faithfulness.

You may now kiss yourself.

Bruised Apples

I buy bruised apples.
I tell them, "It's not your fault."
End spousal abuse.

The Redhead

Eating out redheads
Is as close as I'll ever get
To the red carpet.

Antidepressants

Antidepressants
If I mix them with quick sand
Do they sink or float?

Jack-in-the-Boxes

Jack-in-the-boxes
When we use one, but it dies,
How will we ever know?

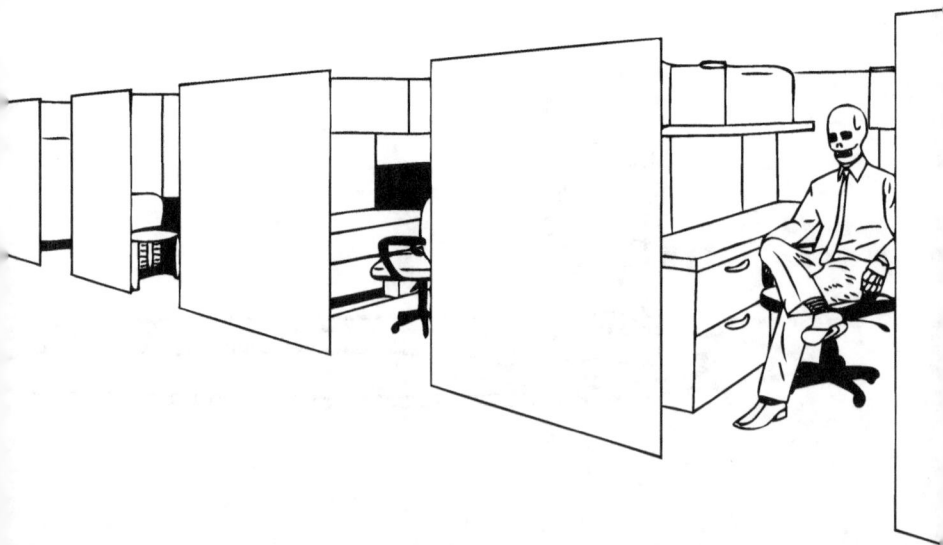

Motivation

Day 1: I can change.
Day 2: I'm feeling better.
Day 3: Meh, fuck this

I Browse

I browse eyebrows.
Not because eyebrows are
> The sign language interpreters of facial expressions,
> The synchronized swimmers of forehead aerobics,
> The sweatshop workers of follicle enterprise.

No, I browse eyebrows because
They are the one true indicator of pubic hair color.

Confounding Father

I saw Ben Franklin
Wandering the streets yesterday.
He was pretty out of it,
Mumbling about hot singles in the area.

I offered him a cab ride,
But he refused,
Because he didn't know what a cab was.
The confusion escalated
When I tried to explain how cabs work,
How saying, "Yo, where your slaves at?" was offensive,
How he didn't need to mail his nudes anymore,
How vaccines were created to prevent diseases,
But some people don't use them.

Ben stood dumbfounded the whole time
Like I had short-circuited his brain.
I gave him my phone and a Tinder profile
And told him to start swiping
While I get help.

When I returned, Ben was gone.
I should have asked that phone-stealer
About the original meaning of the Constitution
When I had the chance.

Soulless

Annez won marathons at any toll,
Using things like shortcuts and bicycles,
Till the bottom of her shoes formed a hole
And Annez realized she had no sole.

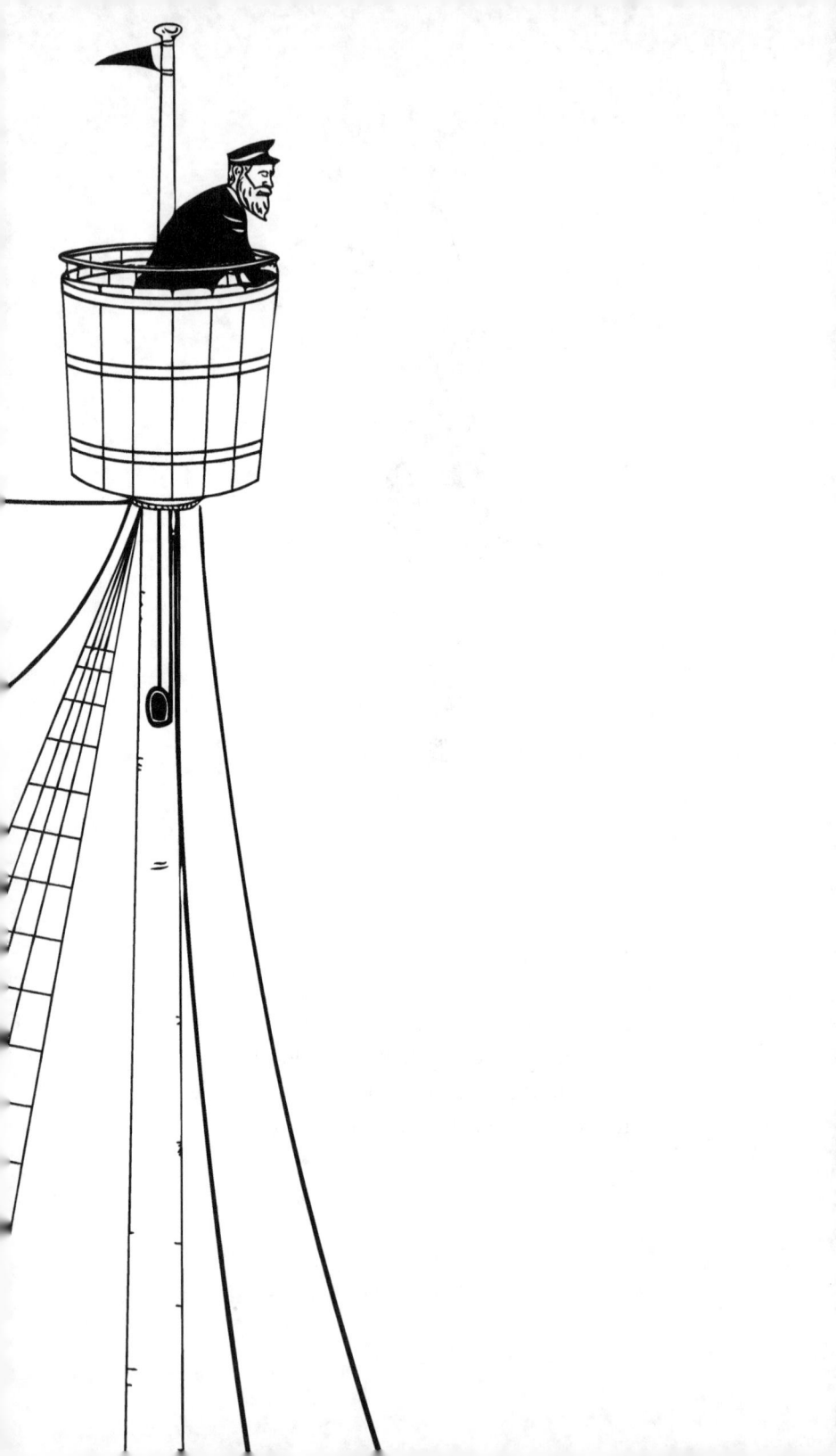

The Search

Captain's Log #538:

Another long day and nothing to show for it. The crew is exhausted. Spirits are low. Deep down I'm starting to have doubts about this rescue mission myself. But I just can't bear the idea of returning to my wife empty-handed.

Whoever A. Life is, they must be important.

The Dive

I stood up on the diving board,
Too scared to move an inch,
Just peering at the pool,
Till my backside felt a pinch.
I fell and fell and fell,
Screaming loud and long,
Till I hit the water and realized
All my fear was gone.

Logorrhea

Silver moon droplets dance on sweet simpering smoke,
Enveloping small footprints along the beaches' edge,
Where kingdoms of virgin fauna once reigned peacefully.
Nearby, a writer's creative license is revoked.

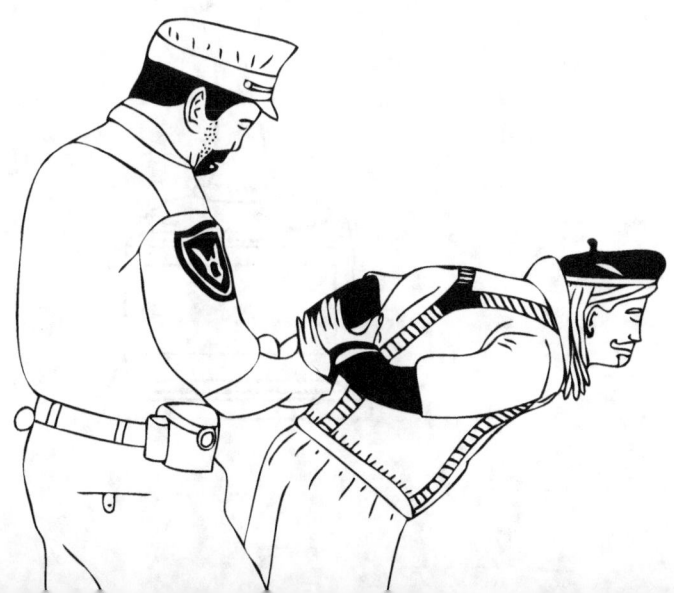

Trophy Wife

I have a trophy wife.
Perfect face, perfect bust.
But my trophy wife doesn't do much.
Her only hobby is collecting dust.

I Knew Love

I knew love
Having read a book or two.
But I didn't feel so smart
The day that I met you.

Samson Stratocaster and Sally Sitar

Samson Stratocaster slunk to class,
Passed troupes of trumpets and bands of brass,
Each stopping to pick on and laugh
At Samson's loosely strung style.

In class, Samson sat in the back, alone,
Tuned out the symphony of Ms. Timpani's drone,
Never spoke a note in his off-key tone,
Unable to see his part in class.

Minutes to hours, hours to days,
Samson stayed muted in de capo malaise
Till, at lunch, Samson caught the suitest gaze
Of Sally Sitar, eating a peanut butter and jam sandwich.

Samson composed himself, but the bell rang above.
Still Sally's signature style was all he could think of.
Resonating like a cymbal, a symbol of love,
Samson knew he had found his masterpiece.

Samson left class half a step out of line,
Chin on his chest, no destination in mind,
Heartstrings plucked by the hands of time,
Till suddenly, Samson bumped into Sally.

Her style was laid back. Her pitch was flat.
Still Sally struck a chord and Samson liked that.
He didn't fret a moment, just started to chat,
Unearthing a duet he'd known all along.

Both loved string cheese, salsas, and stars.
Both admired the stylings of Stephen Stills on guitar.
Both knew they'd found what they'd only seen from afar.
That no matter your tune, there's a key to harmony.

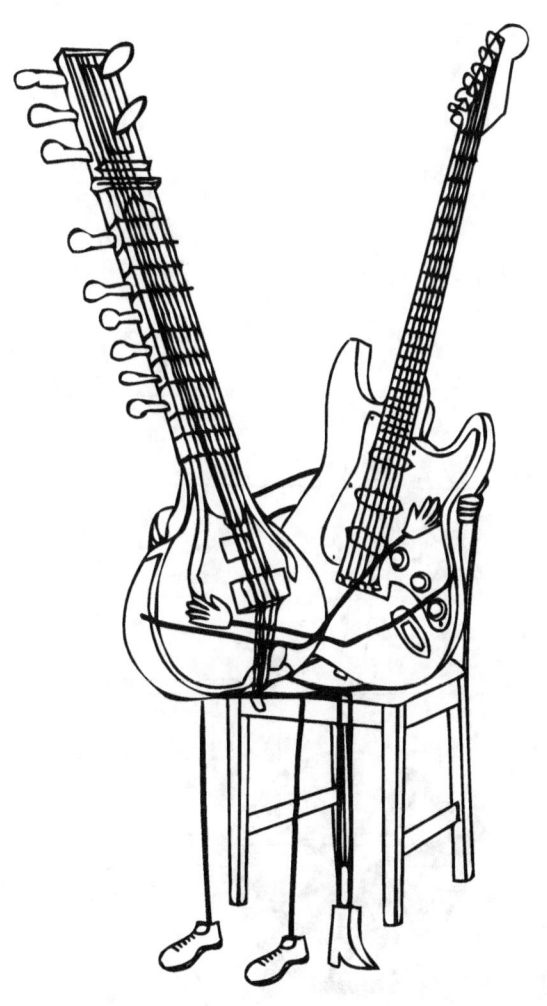

I'm Sorry I'm Late

I'm sorry I'm late. I got stuck in traffic.

I'm sorry I'm late. Assassins dressed as Jehovah's Witnesses attacked my parents and I had to fight them off with a pool noodle.

I'm sorry I'm late. A giant condor abducted me while I was about to cure glaucoma and dropped me in Siberia where I lived off the land selling snow cones until I could afford a sled ride home.

I'm sorry I'm late. My parents were killed in front of me and, after mastering several different martial arts, I dedicated my life to fighting crime in the suit of a flying mammal while simultaneously upholding my image as a playboy billionaire philanthropist.

I'm sorry I'm late. I didn't know this was so important to you.

How to Write a Poem

Line one: get reader's attention.
Line two: expand what's mentioned.
Line three: a couplet's fine.
Line four: just make it rhyme.
Line five: develop themes.
Line six: get more caffeine.
Line seven: insert a twist.
Line eight: retract if reader's get pissed.
Line nine: tie loose ends together.
Line ten: insert something clever.

The Uncatchable Bird

The uncatchable bird
Has never been caught.
More moves than a contortionist.
More slippery than snot.
Many will try to catch it
Across all time
Till one day the hunters
Finally find
That the uncatchable bird
Is a Sisyphean curse,
But damn wouldn't it be awesome,
If they caught it first?

My Problems

I stuck my problems in the closet,
Threw away the key,
But somehow they escaped
And now they're chasing me.

So I pushed my problems in a well,
Figured I was done,
But they managed to get out,
And again I'm on the run.

What started as a nuisance
Has turned into a war
And if my problems ever catch me,
Then that will make one more.

Lunatics

Be vigilant of lunatics.
They are all around us.
The problem is they can be disguised as regular people.
Yesterday, I saw a woman eating pizza crust first.
That's the kind of person we should be watching out for.

Invisible Prisons

The prisons are overcrowded.
There's one on every street
Filled with men and women
Undeserving of the beat.
These prisons don't have bars,
Guards or wired fence,
And folks are welcomed in
Without a criminal offense.
The beauty of the system
Is prisoners needn't stay,
But still they come in droves
From 9 to 5 each day.
The suits aren't always orange.
The meetings don't end in gore.
But the duration of the visits
Are usually forty years or more.
There won't be three square meals though.
Every bathroom will be shared.
And if behavior is outstanding
More work will be prepared,
Until life has slipped away
And the clock strikes a final notch,
Prisoners receive a handshake
And a golden parting watch.
But no matter what the watch says,
No matter how they spent their time,
Prisoners wish their pasts were different,
That they'd pursued a life of crime.

I Hate Cyclists

I hate cyclists
Hogging the roads.
Making me 10 seconds later to my job
That I already hate.
Fuck 'em and their perfectly toned legs.
Fuck 'em testing my reflexes
And my patience.
Fuck 'em all.
Don't they have anything better to do
Than be outside and be healthy?
Worst are the leisurely cyclists.
Lacking pedal speed like a one-handed meth vendor.
The next time I drive by a cyclist,
I'm gonna honk once
As long as it won't confuse other drivers.
That will show them.

Important Message

Hey!
You!
Yes, you!
This is future you.
I need your help! Immediately!
I don't have time to explain why I chose to write this message in a poetry book.

Put $10,000 cash and an iced vanilla latte (don't skimp on the caramel (I'm sure you knew that though)) in an unmarked bag. Place the bag under the bench at 8th and Broadway by 10 a.m. tomorrow.

Hurry! Your future depends on it.

Sincerely,

- You

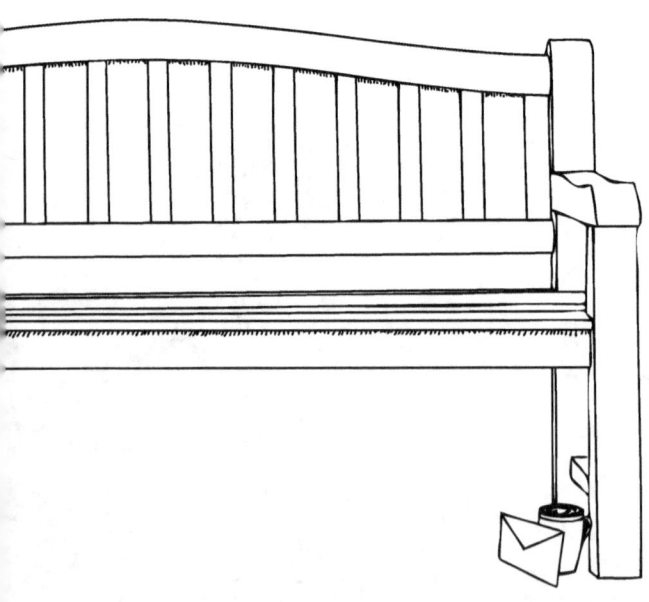

The Cycle

Buy it. Push it. Sell it. Grow it. Cop it. Bust it. Jail it. Detract it. Break it. Shame it. Debt it. Free it. Try it. Bear it. Fail. Relapse it.

The World is Falling Apart

Fire, wheel, civilization,
Agriculture, domestication,
Tools, language, writing, art.
The world is falling apart.

Lights bulbs, AC, vaccination,
Pasteurizing, refrigeration,
Batteries, matches, cotton gin.
The world is in a tailspin.

Cameras, Bluetooth, commercial planes,
Social media, video games,
Computers, phones, GPS.
The world is a total mess.

AI, smart homes, life on Mars,
Time travel, holograms, flying cars,
Teleporting across the universe.
The world now is at its worst.

405

From 9 to 5 to 405
Car Parcheesi without a prize.
Red lights, headlights,
Stoplights, head's light,
Running on empty, trying to fight
The tired, the exhausted, the gassed
Where moving only are minutes passed.
Cruise control without control
A break broken by brakes felt,
If I didn't know better I'd say
Seat belts only protect us from ourselves.

The Most Evil Players

The most evil players are easy to spot.
Mr. and Mrs. Evil wear big smiles.
People call those devils role models.
The Evils help people,
            including you.
They compliment your hustle,
Lend a hand when you're down,
Make you feel wanted.
The Evils make you wonder,
"Why is coach riding my ass?
Obviously someone appreciates the effort?"
Then you'll wonder why your significant other
            has you sleeping on the couch.
The Evil would give you their bed.
The Evils are the best.
Meanwhile, Mr. Evil just made
        the game-winning shot
                over a sap,
                    who let his guard down.

Supervillains

America loves an underdog,
A likeable loser against all odds.
The biggest underdog is a supervillain
With dreams they are never fulfilling.
Supervillains never win
To their perpetual chagrin.
Always booed. Always sneered.
They're singled out for being weird.
Stripped of glory whenever close.
All alone when they need love most.
With tolerance preached for every man,
It's time today we take stand.
If you see supervillains with shoulders shrugged,
Make sure to stop and give them a hug.

A Thin Line

There's a thin line between
Saying and slaying.
Paying and playing.
Fight and flight.
Fat and flat.
Receiving Ana and receiving anal.
You get the idea.

I Wonder If You Think of Me

I wonder if you think of me
When walking through our memories.
Those beautiful moments
Our firsts and lasts
Now buried beneath cranial cobwebs.
I wonder if you think of me
Like I think of you,
An indelible mark
Like red wine on a wedding dress.
Because when you said goodbye
You took a piece of my heart
And I haven't found a replacement since.

Dave and His Bongos

Dave was inexplicitly attracted to his bongos.
He couldn't quite understand why but he was.
Maybe it was the bongos' endless curves or flawless skin.
Perhaps it was the perfect hourglass shape.

"Boink boink," said the bongos.
"I don't know if I can tonight," said Dave.
"Boink, boink, boink."
Dave tried to avoid eye contact.

"Boink, boink."
"But I'm a human. You're a set of bongos. It won't work."
"BOINK, BOINK,"
The bongos' patience was starting to run thin.

"Boink, boink, boink, BOINK"
"What would people say if they saw us together?"
"Boink BOINK boink"
"I don't care if you wear protection or not."

Dave hung his head, too embarrassed to look up.
The bongos recognized this and broke the silence.
"C'mon Dave. One time changes nothing.
I blew a flute today. That doesn't make me bi-instrumental."

Regrettable Events in History

Dawn of man: Adam and Eve decide to listen to a talking serpent instead of the divine word. Mess up eternal paradise for everyone.

1812: Napoleon invades Russia during the winter. Immediately regrets decision.

1890-1927: Movie producers keep forgetting to add sound to films.

1909: Rose lets go of Jack in the *Titanic*. Fool! He loved you! You two were so perfect together!

1920-1933: Prohibition

1980 to 1989: Including, but not limited to jorts, synthesizers, the invention of Bud Lite, denim, a terrible *Jaws* sequel, every hairstyle, sea monkeys, another terrible *Jaws* sequel and no Internet.

2002: Crocs

2012: A hangover so bad I felt Lord Voldemort's presence.

2201: Astronaut Beef Johnson accidentally impregnates alien escort. Intergalactic courts force him to pay child support for every one of the 5,847 fertilized eggs.

The Loneliest People

A truck driver pulls into a tollbooth in western Antarctica.

"God. I haven't seen another person in ages," the tollbooth operator thought. "I would totally fuck his brains out."

"What?" said the truck driver. "I didn't catch that."

"Uh, nothing. Fifty cents please."

Reading Between the Lines

"Hey babe! How are you? My weekend was crazy."
"I binge watched TV and the bedsores didn't faze me."

"I'm good. I was busy both days."
"Spending my time in a sugar induced hazed."

"Nice. Let's get gazpacho. You know? Cold soup."
"Because you fit in those pants like an ice cream scoop."

"Alright. I'm down to try something new."
"Assuming that you're picking up the bill too."

"By the way, I have a little surprise."
"She hates surprises, but a ring should be wise."

"Wow! You shouldn't have. Call me impressed."
"If this is a ring, I'm going to fake my own death."

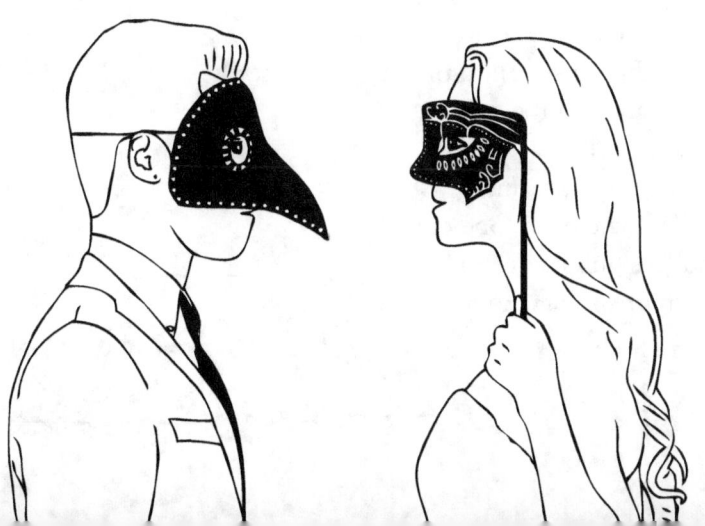

The American Dream

We're told to believe in
The American Dream
When the reality is
It's not what it seems.
We're told the dream's fair
But it's anything but
When the starting point
Is a matter of luck.
We're told with hard work
We can go any place,
But never of the hurdles
That come with the race.
Where colors are equal
Only in mind
As some are more likely convicted
Of victimless crimes.
More likely to imprisoned,
More likely to be poor,
More likely to be pieces
In political war.
The dream is a dream
Where the rich get richer
Leaving the rest
In a growing wealth fissure.
The elected fail to help
Those they're sworn to protect,
While ignoring the poverty
Breeding criminal sects.
So forget the dream,
Throw the current one out,
And let's build a dream
Worth dreaming about.

She

We met freshman year of high school.
I was a windmill of elbows and knees.
She, an untamable siren.
A friend introduced us thinking we would click.
He was right.
I couldn't stay away.
Everyday after school, I would rush to meet her.
We went everywhere.
Just her, me, and the open road.
The possibilities were endless.
But there were obstacles.
Times I wanted to leave.
Moments of doubt.
But the highs — oh man — those euphoric highs.
Those crisp autumn mornings we spent together
with the park to ourselves.
The people we met.
The places we saw.
The way she molded me into the person I am today.

It makes me wonder whether it's running
cross-country or my wife that's the mistress.

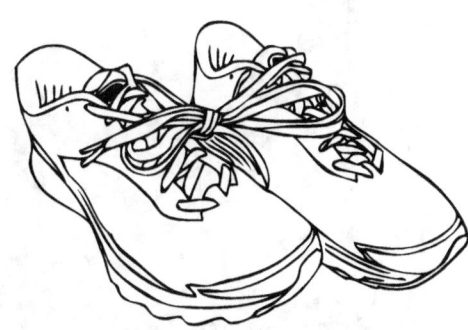

The No Fun Club

I call to order The No Fun Club
To stop writers who make readers feel dumb.

I doth protest your old English.
No sense does it make.
How do I loathe thee?
Let me count the ways.

One, thy lofty language reaches kin,
But the self-importance is wearing thin.
You're two serious and three verbose
Saying "Invisible Man" instead of "ghost."
So to pompous writers, number four,
Quoth the people, nevermore.

The Three Bad Words

On the fringe of town where decency ain't,
Live three bad words that make "Fuck" look like a saint.

Meet Mr. R, Mr. N, and Mrs. C.,
Satan's archangels of profanity.

They turn well-meaning sentences into abuse
Then sneak into jail and let all "Hell" break loose.

These words are evil; they're too vile to say,
But are they naturally bad or did we make them that way?

I Want to Live in Space

I want to live in space,
To enjoy life at a leisurely pace,
Away from the orbit of the global rat race,
Oh yes, I want to live in space.

Space doesn't have traffic, pollution or crime.
I could smoke astroturf all of the time.
I'll trade my whole world for the peace of mind.
Oh yes, I want to live in space.

I'll miss my family without a doubt.
I'll miss five cheese pizza and chocolate stouts.
Still I'm willing to live without.
Oh yes, I want to live in space.

Character

Building character: some assembly required

Reid Reed

Reid Reed couldn't read.
The warning signs he didn't heed.
So when Reid walked in the women's latrine,
It was the most well-red he's ever been.

My Head is Very Heavy

I took a nap and just awoke,
But hardly feel like the same ole bloke.
Am I in the future or is this a joke?
'Cause my insides feel full of concrete.
My head is very heavy.

I wish I remembered what my cousin said,
Those important words while I lay in bed.
Should I dread being dead from this lead-filled head?
Or were his words precautionary?
My head is very heavy.

Oh no! I'm slipping! My head's begun to fall.
I'll surely make a mess upon the floor and on the wall.
Oh, help me!
God!
Oprah!
Biggie Smalls!
Aaaaaagggghhhh!
It's happening! My head has begun to rise.
My head is very light.

I remembered, guys! So death must wait.
Here is the answer to avoid a grisly fate,
You see, around here, your head gains weight
The more that sex is on your mind.
My head is very heavy.

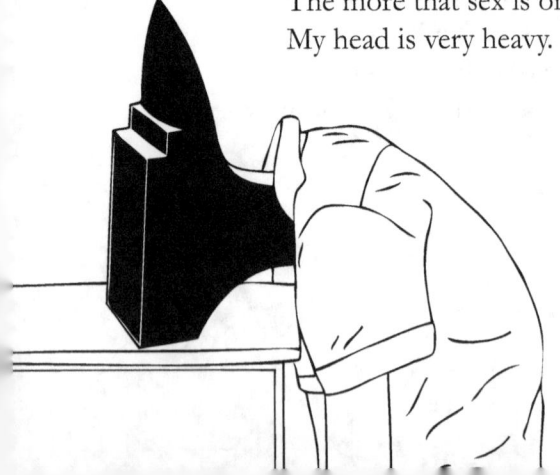

Boyfriend Land

Welcome to Boyfriend Land. The global leader in female orgasms since 2284.

Boyfriend Land has top of the line boyfriends. Each tailored to meet your personal needs.

Take The Chad. Designed for women ages 18 to 25. He's great for everything from sharing gossip to long phone calls with your mother. Plus The Chad doesn't go off with his friends because he needs "personal space." In fact, The Chad looks forward to going down on your "personal space." Best of all, he has a greater emotional availability than his live counterparts.

Need something even more sophisticated? With a simple upgrade, The Chad becomes The Chadwick. Just install the housework chip and you'll have yourself a trophy husband.

So come on down to Boyfriend Land.

The search for Mr. Right ends here.

Perspective is Everything

Perspective is everything.

Some treat vacuuming like a necessity.

Some treat vacuuming like a chore.

Some treat vacuuming like the manifestation of Satan himself because they are dogs and some ninny wanted to vacuum while they were sleeping on the couch.

Happy

If I'm running low on happiness,
I'll buy a loaf from the shelf.
Though it's never quite as good
As the stuff I make myself.

Places and Memories

Of all the places
I have ever been,
There is nowhere
I'd rather be than with you.

And of all the memories
I have ever made,
The sweetest ones
All have you.

While these memories
Had their time,
Still I find them
On my mind.

And I'd give away
All their joy
To avoid the pain
Of remembering you.

All these places that I visit
Are now just markers of the past.
Bittersweet reminders
Of love that did not last.

That's Life

When you eat a popular cereal,
But it tastes like cardboard.
That's life.

When you win an argument,
But end up paying for sex again.
That's strife.

When you fight the red coats,
But play an instrument.
That's fife.

When you go to the bathroom,
But you see a lump.
That's probably a baby.
Or cancer.
Either way, you should get that checked out.

How to Look Busy at Work

- Check your email.

- Take up smoking for the breaks.

- Fake phone conversations.

- Write a list of way to waste time at work.

- Check your email again. Then send emails to yourself.

- Spike your lunch with crippling amounts of laxatives.

- Change religion based on upcoming holidays.
    Whoo, Kwanzaa!

- Count the number of holes in the perforated ceiling tiles.

- Delete the computer's operating system. Claim you're having technical difficulties.

- Ask a lot of questions: Where are the project files? How is your ex-wife? Do you know any remedies for herpes? Asking for a friend, of course.

- Stare intently at computer screen. A hand on your chin helps.

- When confronted with a task, ask, "How urgent is this? These holes in the ceiling tiles aren't going to count themselves."

- Read the terms and conditions.

- Wear stilettos. Men too. If you're going to walk, might as well do it slowly.

- Instead of emails, handwrite every message in calligraphy and hand deliver with fresh wax seal of the company coat of arms.

- Check your email one more time. Look at that, you got an invitation to a Kwanzaa party!

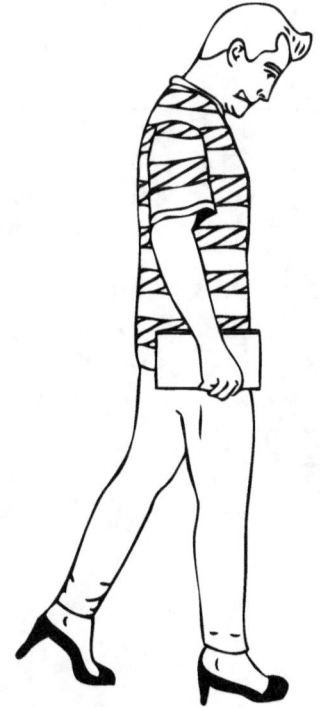

Can We Know?

Can we know war
Without knowing peace?
West without east?
Beauty without beast?

Can we know joy
Without knowing pain?
Loss without gain?
Difference without same?

Can we know freedom
Without knowing oppression?
Self without expression?
Answers without rhetorical questions?

Criminals

Not all criminals wear masks.
Some wear suits. Some wear casts.
Some wear socks and sandals.

Not all criminals are seen.
Some are hackers. Some are thieves.
Some wear too much cologne.

Not all criminals get put away.
Some get wrist slaps. Some get paid.
Some get rum-raisin ice cream.

Then there's you. You heartless wench.
You stole my breathe with just hello.
Now your voicemail is all I know.

The Life Cycle

A partially eaten pastry is thrown into a dumpster bin.
Local flies see the pie and swarm the abandoned tin.

A crowd forms as news gets out, each fly's trying to get a bite,
Cutting at the carcass till dead air fills the site.

What the flies don't know is there's treasure beneath their feet,
Garbage bags of uneaten pastries customers didn't eat.

With a little extra digging, hard work and overtime,
The flies could uncover this life-defining find.

But the flies just skim the surface, content with easy lunch,
Passing chances to change their life because crumbs are good enough.

Anti-Lobby Lobbyist

I am a type of lobbyist,
But not the kind you fear.
Instead of eliminating policy,
I eliminate my peers.

I'm an anti-lobby lobbyist,
The first one ever known,
Taking out the bad guys
Like real life *Home Alone.*

And when the dust has settled
And politics aren't run by wealth.
I'll have my toughest task:
Eliminating myself.

Fishing For Compliments

I'm at my favorite fishing spot
Casting lines with reels of patience,
But the compliments that I've caught
I release without hesitation.

Maybe I should change my game,
My bait or my location,
Because every fishing trip feels the same
Save the declining expectations.

You'd think I'd be less picky
Instead of carrying on,
But my situation's sticky
When every compliment is from my mom.

The Rain

The rain came pouring down
And washed away my wisdom.
Then my shoes, my shirt, my car,
My doubts and disposition.

The rain washed away my fears.
It took my worries too.
Now that I've got nothing left,
I feel good as new.

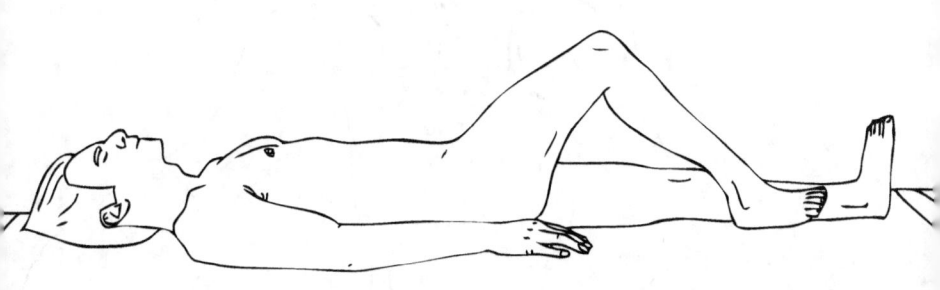

Nice Guys

To ladies who've dated bad boys,
And like to fool around,
Who now want a nice guy
With a passion for going down.

To ladies looking for a cure
Like salami or a doctor,
Who want to find the love
That wasn't given by their father.

To ladies who want a special someone
Who works and cleans and cooks.
Good luck trying to find him.
He's in the last place you'll ever look.

A Thousand Little Pieces

With a glimpse into the past,
I fell into a thousand little pieces,
Shards of my soul scattered about
Like sand in ocean breezes.

I thought I had recovered.
I thought I was just fine,
But your face brought a tidal wave
Of memories back to mind.

Once the flood is over
And my wishful thinking too,
I'll need some time alone
And a ton of superglue.

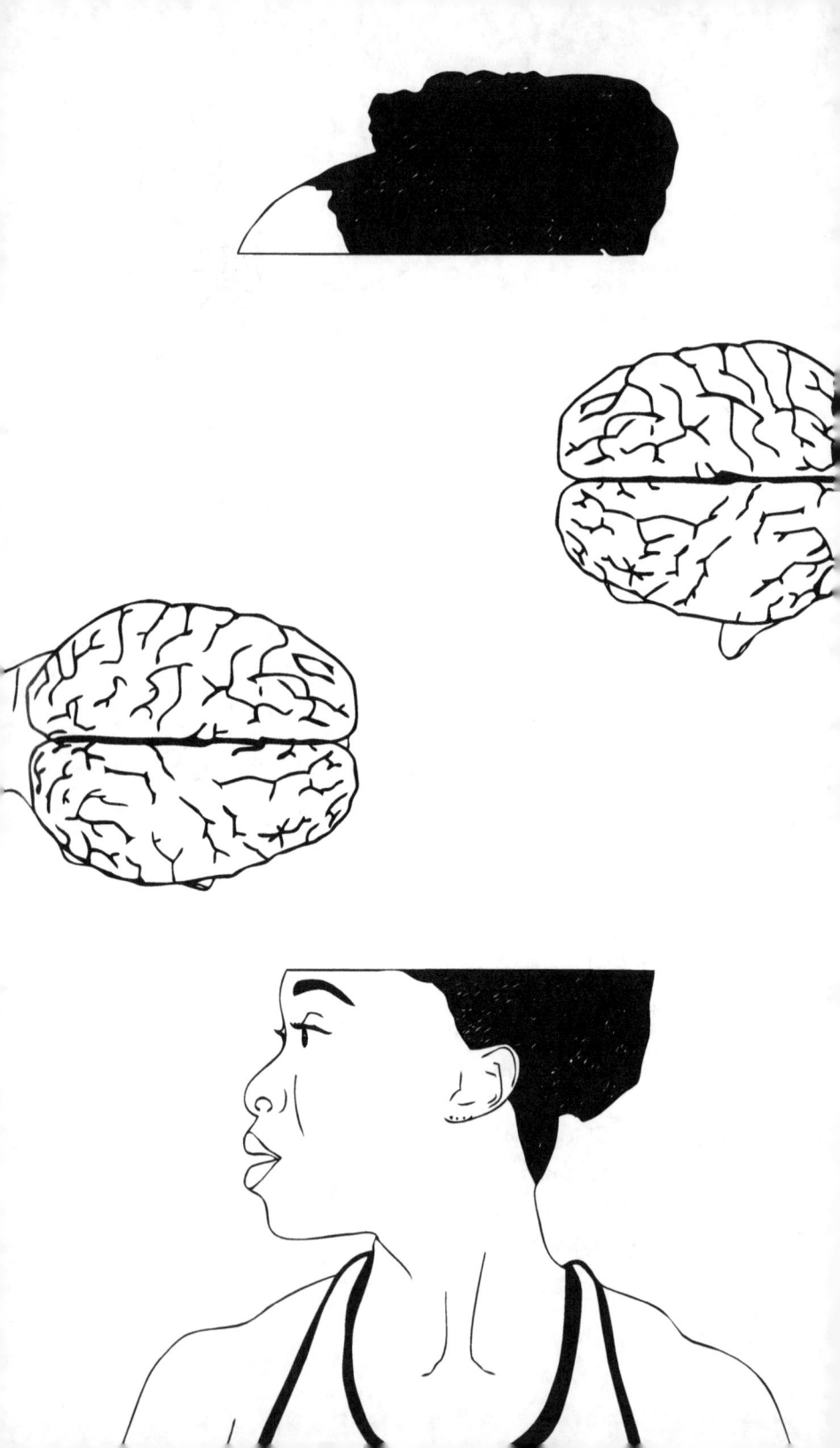

Open-Minded

Eliza is open-minded.
She has a hole on top her head
Where the only thoughts she has
Are those she's heard and read.

Eliza is agreeable.
She regurgitates what she's fed.
If you don't like what she's thinking
Give her different thoughts instead.

Eliza is obedient,
Because she's never had control.
To see there's more to life
Than believing what you're told.

Time Factory

I work at a factory
Making time around the clock.
Moments, minutes, months,
The conveyor never stops.

People never get enough,
Asking me for an hour more.
But I simply smile and say,
"We only make 24."

Happy Father's Day

Father's Day praise is overdone
By dogmatic daughters and Stockholmed sons.
Because with millions of fathers,
I am a doubter
That your dad is really number one.

The Glass House

Lilly bought a glass house
To stay warm inside all year.
But the benefits beyond that
Surely ended there.
If she fought with her kids,
Her neighbors knew.
When she sniffed old laundry,
People screamed, "EWWWW!"
When she got out of the shower,
The little boys oohed.
When she didn't recycle,
Everyone booed.
Now people in glass houses
Know never to throw stones.
The only surefire fix
Is to try and sell their home.

Pencil Factory

Inside every pencil
There's a factory to engage.
All it takes to start
Is contact with a page.

So while an author writes,
Workers build sentences to send,
Placing them on conveyors
And pushing them out the end.

Sometimes the workers bungle
Words they do not know.
When they guess the spelling wrong,
Ta-da, there is a typo.

The factory is always running
Until the writing is at an end.
Then the workers head for home
Until they're needed once again.

Writer's Block

When good ideas are low in stock,
Buy yourself some writer's block.
Chip and chisel, carve and whittle,
Like diabetics eating peanut brittle.
And with some patience, time and drive,
You'll find your masterpiece inside.

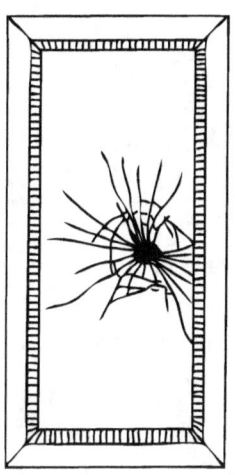

I Hate Him

I hate him.
The puzzle piece smile,
The paper-mâché personality,
The concealed crow's feet
Standing over the void
Where character should reside.
Look at that sad schmuck standing there
With jellyrolls
That turned to belly rolls.
The facial Braille
Silently calling out for help.
The ocular constitution so flimsy
He cannot even hold eye contact.
I hate him.

Good thing reflections aren't real.
Otherwise I'd put him out of his misery.

Love Struck

For every arrow Cupid shoots
Comes a lesson to impart,
Like how a major change in life
Can come from a minor change of heart.

A) Yesterday, Cupid shot a man
Killing him without a fight,
Which just goes to show
Don't sleep with Cupid's wife.

B) Yesterday, Cupid shot a chainsaw
Who fell in love with a tree,
Which just goes to show
Some loves aren't meant to be.

C) Yesterday, Cupid shot a bat
While a mole was passing by,
Which just goes to show
Sometimes love is blind.

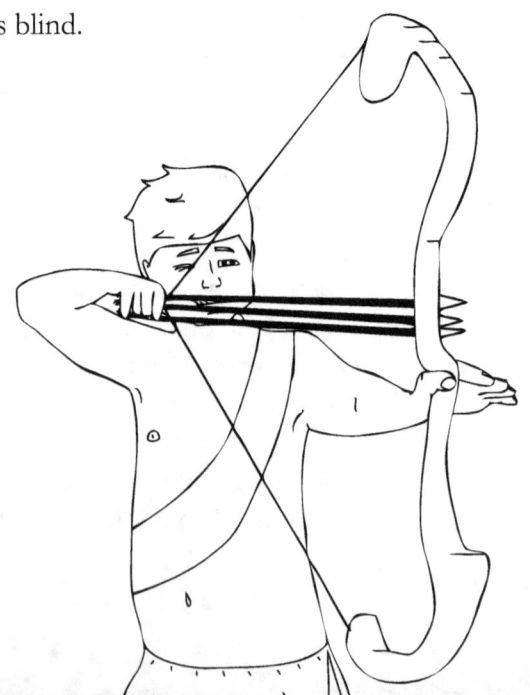

Trail Blazing

My shadow wanted more
Than to follow in my footprints.
So he packed his bags,
Said goodbye,
And has made his own path ever since.

Searching for Soulmates

Searching for soulmates
By swiping online
Is like buying a house
Without looking inside.

Passed good and better
Content only with best
As if a squeaky doorknob
Ruins the rest.

And when the last house makes
Somebody's dream,
A doorbell is the closest
You'll get to a ring.

The Robins

The robins longed to ride the breeze,
To sail along the silver seas,
To go wherever the winds or whims pleased,
And leave the nest far behind.

Then right before graduation
The robins learned about deforestation,
About Avian disease and predation,
Clipping the sensation of how wonderful freedom would be.

The life of robins is full of stress,
Everyday a fight for food, shelter and rest.
Robins must be smart to survive outside the nest,
But it's the smartest robins that never left.

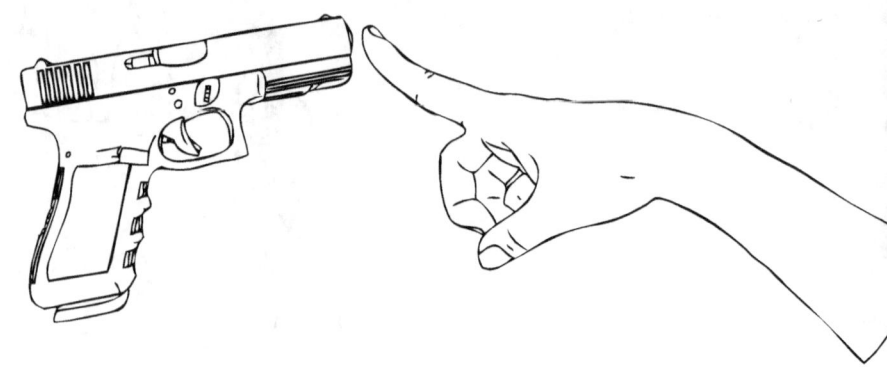

Fuck the Police

Fuck the police.
There I said it.
Their taxpayer salaries. Fuck 'em.
Their donut-induced diabetes. Fuck 'em.
Their irregular hours that make raising a family nearly impossible.
Fuck 'em.
Fuck the police long and hard.
In fact, let's spit roast them
      with the system they are obligated to uphold,
      but doesn't serve the people's best interests.
Yessir, a pity fuck is the least we can do.

Pity Party

I had a pity party
And invited all my friends.
A catharsis for a narcissist
And his self-deprecating pen.

I played pin the blame and spin the truth,
Amassing pity until the end.
But none of my friends showed up.
Now I pity them.

Complimentary Reviews

Imagine if restaurants
Had complimentary reviews,
Where the reviews aren't for the restaurants.
The reviews are for you.

Customers would get scored
During every dining trip
From how much bread they eat
To their average total tip.

The reviews would get specific
Like, can you use chopsticks?
Do you eat pizza with a fork
Or think filet mignon's a type of fish?

Restaurants need complimentary reviews,
But they simply don't exist.
They can only hope customers follow the golden rule:
Please don't be a dick.

Seeing Color

"Oh, I don't see color," said Jay,
His eyes hostage to shades of grey.

Making his mismatched socks look the same
And Twister an impossible game.

To Jay, "go" is the signal at every light
And his fruits and vegetables are always ripe.

And as my broker, Jay said I was set,
But where he saw green, I was in debt.

Now, Jay might not see color, though I find it odd,
That he started seeing red when I sued for fraud.

Nigerian Prince

I'm a Nigerian prince.
My wealth I long to share.
But no one answers my emails
To make them a millionaire.

Diamonds

I
do
not
like
these
prices.
Buying
diamonds
maximizes
financial
hardness.
Virtues
stones
merit
over
you
or
I

I Walked In On My Grandparents

I walked in on my grandparents having sex.
Methodically fucking as if time did not apply.
The sound of their smacking flesh
Filling the increasingly dusty room.

Every thrust and caress was calculated
For this slow motion ballet of debauchery,
Stopping only to savor the bodily nectars
As if to suggest these are wasted on the youth.

Was there meaning in grandparents fucking?
Some symbolism perhaps?
If there was, I missed it.
I got out of there in a flash.

Happy Ending

Every story cannot have a happy ending.
Sometimes Mother Nature is a cold-hearted bitch.
Sometimes she fucks with people for her own amusement.

That's life.

Get over yourself, rose petal.

Cell Phones

There is a place where the sun starts in the west,
Where there's division by zero and low scores are best.*
There is a place where fairytales roam
And humans live in pockets worn by cell phones.

Here every phone has a human at least a cords-length away,
A cellulite morphine used everyday.
Where phones live on a pleasure that's a battery kill,
Even though humans are meant to fulfill.

You see, humans here have an ironic complexion
Making believe instead of connecting,
And in the world where humans service machines,
The real question is: who's pulling whose strings?

*except for golf

Princess Paige

Princess Paige had a lisp.
So she searched her kingdom for a fix.
"H-h-help," she stammered,
"And I'll make you, uh, rich."

Princess Paige got her wish.
The lip twisting slips forever nixed.
People came together for her sake,
And burned her for being a witch.

The Bachelor

Time is short and odds are long
To find a person with whom you belong.
Because with love today a swipe away
Too many people search and say,
"Meh, I can do better."

But if you're like me and don't care to bother,
If your only self-esteem comes in the sauna,
Or if your nicer genes are with your brother,
Just wait. Take a number.
A little patience goes a long way.

Because when iron hearts succumb to rust,
When expectations lie beneath veils of dust,
When internal clocks are set to rest,
When people want whatever's left.
Baby, you've got a one-way ticket to a lifetime fuckapalooza.

A World Without Wi-Fi

My dad's bedtime stories
Give me nightmares to this day.
Tales about a world
Where the Wi-Fi went away.

Where chat rooms were in person,
Where Fishers referred to Carrie,
And if you needed answers,
There was a thing called a library.

A world without Wi-Fi
Is a world without connection.
My dad had a different word.
He called it, "perfection."

You Might Not Like

You might not like this poem.
You might not like this book.
If you go to UNC,
You probably don't like Duke.

Well, if that's the way it is,
If I'm the spicy to your mild,
I have one last word to say,
And that word is: SMILE!

Seriously though. Smiling can increase your life expectancy
(I think) and make you more attractive to potential partners.
No sense in being a Frederick Frownyface.

Here, let's do lip calisthenics together.

Ready?

Begin.

One and two and three and smile.
One and two and three and…

I Live on a Boat

I live on a boat
On Lake
St. Clair.
It's heaven if heaven's
On a
Rocking chair.
My boat's great for joyrides
Not cutting
Hair
And when it comes to seclusion
Nothing
Compares.

Every meal is fresh
If you like
Eating shoal
And bathes are a snap
Until the lake
Gets cold.
For each of these highs
There are
Equal lows,
But when you live on a boat
That's how
It goes.

The Perfect Person

The perfect person doesn't exist,
They're a colloquial fairytale. A cultural myth.

The perfect person requires incongruous parts,
To be strong and decisive, yet humble and smart,
To know science and math, yet Dali and Descartes,
To know the place where each roll of tape starts.

The perfect person will never be found,
To fit in with squares while being perfectly round,
To reach new heights without leaving the ground,
To eat chips in the theater without making a sound.

The perfect person will never be seen,
But when I'm with you, I've got the next best thing.

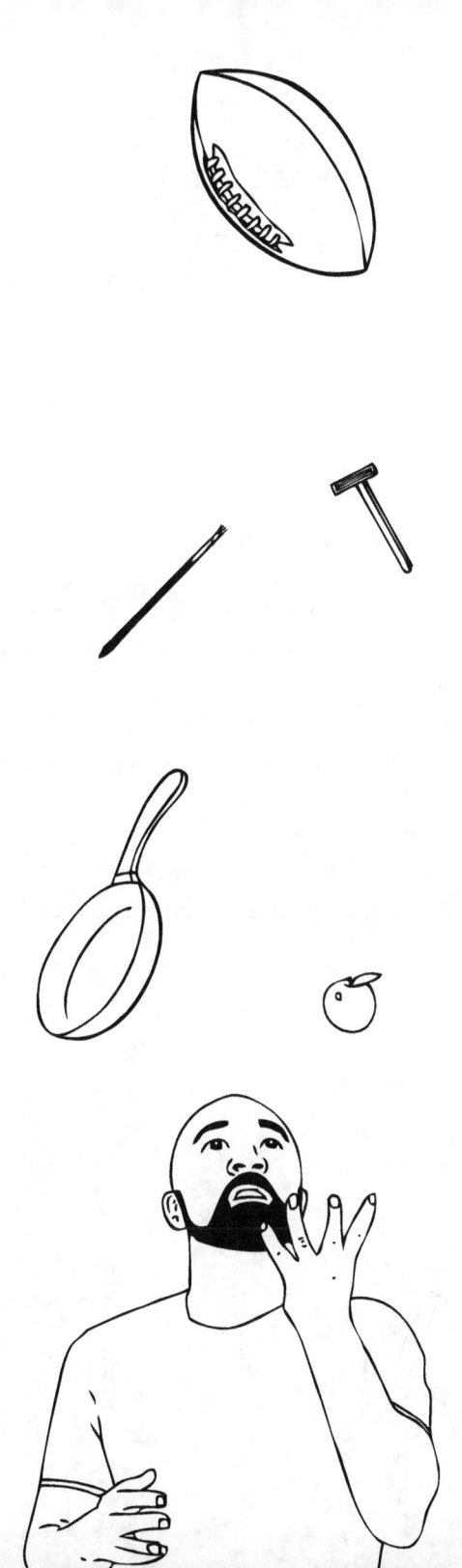

Golden Years

Golden years are wasted on the elderly.
What a crime to be imbued with such contentment.
As soon as the elderly slip the shackles of corporate servitude,
they trade their newfound freedoms for shuffleboard and
discount margaritas.
What a waste.
Riding the coattails of retirement into a garden-variety sunset.
Nature's call falls on deaf ears,
        or at least those hard of hearing.
The elderly are good with good enough.
But how can you argue with discount margaritas?

Zombies

Zombies listen, but never hear
Because words don't stay between zombie ears.
Zombies read, but never think
Because zombie brains are just like sinks.
Zombies live, but never learn
Because zombie memories are one big blur.
Zombies take, but never give
Because a zombie can't die if it's never lived.

Reincarnation

If life is a game
Where points are awarded,
What are they worth
If the game gets restarted?

We Are Gathered Here Today

I've never try to be a nice guy,
Because I know that when I die
People will visit my grave
And my name they'll praise,
Because I'll offer free Wi-Fi.

Heaven's Gate

Why does heaven have a gate?
Who is being kept out?
Or, is heaven keeping people in?
A gate seems pretty pretentious.
Is heaven the gated community of the afterlife?
And why is there only one person checking everyone in?
I want answers.

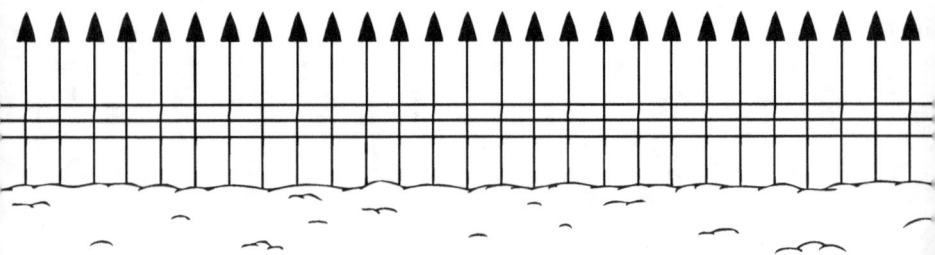

The End

For every idea that I get,
A light bulb lights up in my head.
But my light bulb won't turn on,
So this must be the end.

Thank you
To my friends and family
To Ali Farokhmanesh for beating Kansas in 2010
To my dogs for thinking I'm way cooler than I actually am
To Bo Burnham and Shel Silverstein for inspiration
To you